Swing, Sashay, Shimmy Away

Short story collection

Willa van Gent

Willa van Gent

Swing, Sashay, Shimmy Away

Short story collection

Impressum

Also by this author:
Blue Butterfly, Angel Wings (2009)
Basketful of Butterflies (2010)
Leap of Faith (2011)
Traces of Love (2011)
Surviving Choppy Seas (2013)
Prickly Pears (2019)
Penguins, Goddesses & Other Ceramic Creations (2020)
Viennoiseries – with CelineK – children's stories,
Vienna by Foot (2020, 2022)

Bibliografische Information der Deutschen Nationalbibliothek:
Die Deutsche Nationalbibliothek verzeichnet diese Publikation in der Deutschen Nationalbibliografie; detaillierte bibliografische Daten sind im Internet über http://dnb.dnb.de abrufbar.

Herstellung und Verlag: BoD – Books on Demand, Bad Ensfeld (DE)

ISBN: 978-3-7568-5742-5

CONTENTS

FRESH BREAD, CLEAN DISHES, CLOSED CURTAINS

First serious boyfriend, first time cooking and cleaning, keeping house for young couple. New city for her, not knowing where bakery or supermarket is, needs to provide fresh bread for breakfast. Improvise reheating day-old bread, dampening a bit with water and heating in oven. He exclaims, after first bite, 'What is this?! This bread is not fresh!' She stammers, attempts to cover the small trick of feigned freshness. 'I always want fresh bread!' he fumes.

A few days later, same situation, this time croissants can be reheated, they come out crispy and warm from oven, Boyfriend bites in and does not notice deception. As he eats away, stress and relief wash over her, she had been expecting another outraged outburst.

Next hurdle came during cleaning up and washing the dishes. She wanted to not use up all the dishwasher detergent, put a few drops only on the dirty plates. Gave them a quick scrub, placed them in the rack to drip-dry. He came into the kitchen, eyed her critically, picked up one of the clean plates, swiped it with his index finger, held the plate up, tilted it back and forth in the light. 'This is not really clean, rinse it again, properly!' he ordered. She rinsed the plate a second time, 'But with more soap and very hot water!' he commanded.

At night, the exterior blinds had to be lowered to the bottom, completely sealing the window, not a glimmer of light, sound or air to seep through. She felt as if she were suffocating, panic attack coming on in that dark, silent room. She was used to the window being open a crack, hearing birdsong in the morning, feeling a fresh breeze come in when all had cooled down outside. She begged him to leave the blind open if only few centimeters, just a tiny sliver, so she could see some light on the floor and imagine she was getting air. 'If I wake up at 5 in the morning because of those loud birds chirping, I will wake you up and throw you out of bed so you close the blinds!' he fumed. Yes yes, she agreed. Next morning at 6, she woke with a start, almost a heart attack, fearful, worried, would he hear the birds or see the first rays of sun?! Quickly she jumped out of bed and lowered the blinds to the floor, to leave the room completely dark again. She did not want to incite his impatience and anger, she wanted to do everything right by him.

Oh the fears of A New Love trying to please the other.   August 1991

5

BRITISH LIT

Last May when I went home to visit my parents, I heard that Miss Alducin had Alzheimer's and was in a home. I could not believe it, my favourite high school literature teacher, she who had tried to make our unripe minds understand the complexities of Macbeth, Pygmalion and the Romantic poets. Like Miss Fonseca, who a few years earlier gave me "Jane Eyre" and "Wuthering Heights," opening a whole new world of struggling young women, fighting against parents and pining for boyfriends, just like me.

'If Miss Alducin is in a home now, who will spread the word of English Literature, who will encourage young students to write, to put pen to paper and order their thoughts into a coherent story?' I thought despondently. Miss Alducin made us watch the 1939 version movie version of 'Wuthering Heights,' swooning over Laurence Olivier and Merle Oberon as protagonists. The movie was in black and white and we barely followed the dialogue, but the magic of seeing these two beautiful young hero and heroine, with their tragic love story, was unforgettable. We did not quite understand it, but Miss Alducin knew our minds would take something good out of it. Bless her knowing heart for that, thank you Miss Alducin!

December 2018

FROM WAR TO JUNGLE

When they diagnosed his cancer, too far along to be eradicated, he knew his months were counted. He saw with clarity the decades he had lived, the countries he visited, the houses where he lived, his two children. In that moment of fragility and fear, he realised he had to go back to her, his first love, his first wife, the mother of his kids, the one he had left for another woman. Foolish and weak, oh the flesh is weak, he sighed.

A man of the cloth, he met his future wife on a ferry crossing the English Channel, from England on the way to France, on his way home to Belize. He was mulato, Creole, dark-skinned with piercing blue eyes, a great beautiful man, clean and clear English, just graduated from Selwyn College in Cambridge. She, a young woman, had started a conversation with him on the ferry. The boat trip passed quickly and once on land in France, they did not want to part company. After that, Daisy never left his side, endured her parents cutting her out of the will because she dared cohabitate with a man of colour. She moved to Belize with him, future archdeacon, tying their two children to the porch posts. Should they venture beyond the terrace, the jungle would swallow them and she would never again see her golden boy and girl.

1941

On another continent, Heinz lay on the grass in the field and thought today may be the day he died. He had written the letter to his wife, giving her the password for the bank account, he knew he had a 4-month old son whom he had only seen in a small black-and-white photograph. If it all ended today out on the edges of Russian fields, he had loved, he had given everything for his country, he hoped one day his wife would remarry and his son grow to be a strong, capable man. Heinz adjusted his glasses and took his machine gun to the front. It was a balmy August day, he was amongst comrades, those shreds of beauty and harmony would be in his thoughts, hoping to shut out the noise of war and death around him. Hopefully in his next life there would be peace, no more war, this could not be the answer, he thought.

1982

From these two men of completely different backgrounds and upbringings sprang a daughter and a son whose paths would cross four decades later, in Mexico City. She was the love child from that British-Belizean union, he was the love child from a double-German idealistic union. She overcame racism because of skin colour, he overcame shaming for his war-rooted background. Would the parents ever have imagined their children growing up on the New Continent, far from Old World prejudices? The scars from the parents' choices were borne by their children.

Daisy's daughter, engaged in her early 20s to a young man from a good Mexican family and fortune, saw her dream of a love match disappear when both sets of parents met for the engagement dinner and his parents saw her mulatto father. 'She is half-black!' his parents whispered in horror. 'Our prodigal son, attractive, university-educated, soon to inherit the family fortune, cannot marry a half-caste!' The engagement was cancelled and Susy never married.

The stigma of darker skin, of races mixing, of love between white and dark skin, was felt by both mother and daughter, decades apart. Daisy's family disowned her, struck her inheritance off the books, punishing her for loving a mulato. Her daughter Susy was punished for the same reason, tragic to see humans have not learned that skin colour is irrelevant and the only important emotion is love. Love, tolerance, patience, acceptance of diversity, celebration of diversity.

Susy recovered from that failed marriage engagement. She went on to celebrate herself, wore bright red lipstick, large clip earrings, smoked, her voice booming across rooms. Susy was brash, forward, opinionated. Her character was perfect for meetings and note-taking, her weekly social column in the local English-language newspaper was read by all. If your name was mentioned in Susy's column, you had arrived, you had landed amongst the *crème de la crème*.

Heinz's son put down a meteoric career in hotelry, going from receptionist all the way to general manager. He met queens, kings, presidents, singers, actors and actresses, all of them stayed in the 5-star hotels he managed.

Footnote: Daisy's daughter died a heroine, trying to save her friend's life. Her downstairs neighbour had seen a strange man at Susy's door, called her and let her know. When Susy arrived and they entered the apartment together, the man was caught red-handed, throwing valuables into large, black garbage bags. He lunged at Susy's friend with a knife, Susy got between them, he killed her. He left the body, tied up, in the apartment. Police caught the man a few months later, he was the lover of Daisy's house-boy, Alberto.

Alberto had served Daisy for years, after her death, he stayed in the apartment, serving Daisy's daughter Susy. Alberto picked up this younger man as a lover, told him about the apartment where he worked, filled with British porcelain and silverware. One afternoon, Alberto brought his lover to the apartment. Dazzled by it all, Lover started packing a few items into a bag, horrifying Alberto. When Alberto expressed his disagreement, Lover killed him, bundled him up and threw the body into the bedroom closet. A few minutes later, Susy and friend were at the door. The robbery went tragically awry, ending in a double homicide. When the police arrived later, they found Susy's body, and after further searching, servant Alberto in the wardrobe.

Susy's brother had died a few months earlier, on a highway accident. With both of Daisy's offspring dead, the brother's widow drove to Mexico City with a van, emptied what was left after the robbery and trucked it up to Manzanillo, where her kids would one day inherit the few English valuables. In a roundabout way, all of Daisy's cherished treasures ended up in the tropical jungle anyway.

November 2019

WAR IBID.

Ilse was 4 when WWII ended. Doctor injected her scalded right foot with an infected needle, as revenge that her mother had called him a 'Nazi' a few weeks earlier. Ilse's foot got infected, there were no medicines, she limped around. The other town doctor said the foot had to be amputated at the ankle. Ilse and her mother travelled to the next town with a hospital, were not taken because soldiers had filled it up. The mother decided this was a sign and she herself would attempt to heal her daughter's foot.

A few days later, American soldiers drove by in a Jeep, called Ilse over, from seeing her playing in the garden. They left a bandage, salve and tiny round tin filled with powdered penicillin, at that time an absolute luxury, something to be found nowhere. Sprinkle it on the wound, they said. A week later they came back with more bandages, salve and another little penicillin tin. By then, Ilse's foot was recovered and they had not even used up the second tin, having enough penicillin on reserve, just in case.

February 2020

DRESS CODE 1

It was a stark black, grey and white meeting room in the office. The interviewing boss sat at one end of the long table, leaning back, vaguely present at this menial task. After asking about skills, delineating working hours, expected tasks and such, he asked, as was form, 'Do you have any questions?'

She asked, 'Is there a dress code?' – thinking, no jeans, no sneakers.

'No real dress code, just do not come in a bikini,' he said.

A bikini?! She would never come to work in a bathing suit, that was obvious, she was not applying for the lifeguard or pool attendant job. It was a city secretarial post. Where was his mind? Freudian slip, he had mentally removed all her clothes and she sat there – in his minds' eye – in a bikini?! Did she want to imagine him in less clothes than that dress shirt and suit pants? No, better stick to the staid, prim office dress code!

September 2003

DRESS CODE 2

The smallish hotel claimed it was a 5-star. Upon closer inspection, the carpets were a bit worn, the mirrors' edges were banged up, the bathrooms were missing a screw or tile here or there. The owner had not invested in ages, staff were kept at a minimum, the property was to be juiced for all it would give, until it would give no more. The staff canteen and changing room were two dark, dank basement chambers, adjoining, so the bad smell from the employee toilet wafted into the eating area every time the door was opened. Even with a tilted window open, a cloud of drainage air hung over the changing room, so that people dressed and fled as quickly as possible. The hotel also saved on uniforms by stating that staff were to wear 'all black,' down to the shoe soles. Earrings on women employees were to be no larger than a $2 coin. When one staffer showed up with a t-shirt under a satin blazer, he was informed that this was too casual, next time with a collar please.

Uniforms financed by staff = cost-saving for the proprietor. Solely the hotel manager could send his 6 shirts for dry-cleaning at hotel expense, picked up every Friday evening, delivered on hangers under plastic sheets the next day. For everyone else, no individual personality to be expressed, only all-black. The two contrasting worlds – luxury rooms above-ground, grimy staff quarters below-ground – were geographically and symbolically far apart. No teaspoons to be found in the staff canteen, and only certain staffers dared wear shirts or blazers that were not black, The Chosen Few, the manager's lover or assistant.

October 2019

HANDSOME FATHER AND SON CAFE

It was a small, tiny space, a dozen seats indoors, six seats outdoors for Spring and Summer. Julian, the owner, was a fiftyish man, grey hair, glasses, favouring bright-coloured pants, red, green, orange. His twentyish son had brown, curly unruly hair which hung over his forehead, trendy, fashionably cool, easy smile. Both men stood behind the counter, serving up frothy lattes and powerful espressi, easy chitchat in between.

Women of all ages and backgrounds flocked to the coffee cubbyhole. A particularly flashy, lipstick-covered, scantily-clad woman past her youth regularly waltzed in, yelling, cooing, 'Hellooo Juuuulllliiiiiaaaannnnn!' as she traipsed herself seductively across a chair, batting her eyelashes at him. 'How are you?!?! How is business this morning?!?! How has your week been?!?!' Julian played it cool, served coffee and counted inventory or advised the sole male client on various coffee bean properties. When the frumpy daughter-in-law was behind the counter, seats remained ghostly empty. Clients were only drinking coffee when the handsome men were making it for them.

On a particularly cold and grey Autumn evening, an hour before closing at 6pm, the cafe had been filled with after-work friends of Julian's, including his younger brother, a professor. Bald, elegant in a suit, matching tie and silk square in the breast pocket, neatly folded into a point, Brother held court on global warming, birth control and internet speed. Another set of handsome brothers listened attentively, their long lashes blinking nobly behind horn-rim glasses. The sporty fifth man in the cafe wore a baseball cap and expensive sneakers, sipping a cool glass of bubbly. Men amongst themselves, relaxing after work, grabbing a quick sip of espresso with oatmeal milk or prosecco, small luxuries during the week.

February 2019

SPICE UP YOUR LIFE

Yesterday, I was walking in U3/U4 Landstrasse from the green line to the orange, to switch to U3 towards Erdberg, morning rush, on way to work. On the wall was one of those electronic poster boards that flash a new ad every few minutes, they had one for spices (oregano, pepper, basil) with the tag line, 'Spice up your life!' I read it, then headed towards the escalator, at that moment an airline pilot walked towards me, got to the top of the stairs and going the other direction. Handsome, elegant, full navy blue uniform with gold buttons, pulling his perfect little carry-on, lightning bolt, I thought, 'Oh yes, that will spice up my life for sure!

May 2019

SMART ELEVATORS

The new elevators cause amusing moments of surprise and quandary. Where before some people waited on purpose 'for the next one,' now the smart keyboard assigns one an elevator, 'If you are going to the 10th floor, the fastest, closest elevator is Elevator D.' While waiting, you see a few interesting people and think you will ride up with them, but no, they have been assigned Elevator B. Where before men used to hold an elevator up to let a last-minute hot arrival join them in the small space, now they only look on in despair, she was assigned to another elevator. Since there are no buttons inside the elevator, no one can control where they are going, when the doors will open or close. No favours to be made, no favourites or disagreeables to let on or block. Technology trumps human desires in the name of speed and efficiency. If you do not want to take the stairs, hand your free will over to the smart keyboard and its elevator assignments. The mechanical voice does not even ask, 'Are you in or are you out?' Doors simply close in a silent whoosh and one is left standing helplessly, staring at the numbers display. Let's try that again.

June 2019

CANARY BIRD ADVICE

Oma married in her twenties, gave birth to two daughters, worked most of her life in stores, factories, offices and at home. She never complained, never kicked her drinking, smoking, raging husband out. Every Sunday she went to Mass in the morning. When she was in her teens, she adopted a stray dog, white with a black patch over one eye. She baptised him Pinky, loved that dog, always wanted another dog after that. Opa forbade it. Only in her 60s did she indulge herself by acquiring a yellow canary bird. She baptised him Hans, kept his cage in the kitchen, by the big window. She talked to Hans, loved hearing him sing.

Every day Hans got fresh sand in his cage, every day Oma said to him, *'Hans, heirat' jo net!'* ('Hans, you better not marry!') Opa hated that bird and hated his wife tell that bird what truly lay in her heart. He was jealous of the bird, getting special attention from *his* wife. On the days that Hans got a bath in the special tub hanging on the cage door, Opa hated that bird even more. Oma delighted in watching Hans splash about, showed that bird more affection than she had shown Opa in the past two decades. If divorce were easier at the time, she probably would have done it, but she grew up during the decades it was considered taboo and a divorced woman might as well consider herself beyond society. So she advised her beloved yellow canary bird, 'For sure do not marry, Hans!'

When the girls were teenagers, over thirty years ago, Opa had gotten a job as barracks manager in Tirol, in the middle of snowy Alps. He installed himself there, expecting wife and both daughters to join him as soon as school was out. When they arrived to visit him, a few weeks into his new job, they realised he had a floosy on the side. Left alone a few weeks and already had a new piece of muslin on his arm. Younger Daughter left quickly, got back to the city and found herself an office job, no way she was moving to Tirol. Oma did the same, arriving in Vienna and finding work. A few months later, Opa arrived, knocking on the door, tail between his legs. Why Oma took him back we will never know, but decades later, she advised her canary bird to stay free.

June 2019

WAR MEMORIES

I am - genetically speaking - the last of a long line of strong women. My sister and I have no children, our only nephew is 12 (who knows if he will have kids, and if one of those will be a woman, a strong woman), so I must write down what I have learned up to now and hope that these words live longer than our own brief lives.

Pa was born May 1941 and Ma was born May 1945. When Ma was born on 30 May 1945, they said she was a '*Friedensbaby*,' peace baby, World War II had just ended a few weeks earlier, on 8 May, with Germany's complete surrender. They named her Elfriede, not because of this, but because her father wanted a son, Friedrich, so when he heard he had a daughter, he feminised what his ideal boy name had been.

Pa remembers his mother taking him to the US soldiers' camp. His mother was widowed in August 1941, her husband never saw his son. As a war widow with a toddler, a few years later, she started dating an Willi, a cook and pastry chef in the German army. After the war, the American army hired him for one of their military camps near Alsfeld (Hesse). As cook, he was not allowed to take food home, but he could bring his family to eat at the camp. Pa has clear memories of American soldiers offering him oranges, bananas, canned luncheon meat and chocolates. Husband#2 was not all smooth sailing. Early into their dating, Liz was going to break it off. he pointed a gun at her and threatened to kill her if she ever left him. They remained together until her death five decades later.

Liz's mother, Wilhelmine, also a war widow (from WWI), never remarried and lived until her death at 72 in 1965 with her daughter and grandchildren. Pa remembers his tough Prussian grandmother, 'tall (169 cms), thin, sharing the bedroom with her 3 grandchildren, being carried out dead wrapped in bed sheets.' She was their mother, since her daughter, mother to Pa and his 2 siblings, had to work most of the time and the grandkids were left in the care of their grandmother.

Wilhelmine's husband, Franz Hugo van Gent, a baker, went off to fight in Flander's Fields, dying during the last days of WWI in Halle, Belgium. He was an only son, one year after he died, his mother passed away, his father 2 years later, probably of grief over their 33-year old son never coming home to them or his wife, never having seen his infant daughter Liz.

Hugo was wounded ("lightly") twice during WW1, the first time in 1915, the second time in 1917. In these pages, his name is amongst the list of the injured.

1st injury – *Verlustlisten* (List of Injured Soldiers) published on 12 November 1915, page 10082

Hugo Franz van Gent – Frintrop, Oberhausen (place of birth), List Preussen (Prussia) 378, Reserve-Infanterie-Regiment 255, Stab des I. Bataillons (part of 1st Batallion), 7. Kompagnie (7th Company), Government ID FRIROPJO31JM – *leicht verwundet* (wounded lightly) (categories were "wounded lightly," "wounded heavily" and "fallen")

```
uffz. Heinrich von Rehm — Straffen, Ulees — leicht
Uffz. Wilhelm Subeck — Schnathorst, Minden —
Gefr. Heinrich Kregel — Naffabel, Kreuzburg — lei
Gefr. Gustav Hauck — Geißelberg, Pirmasens — gef
Getr. Stanislaus Lubeck — Samter — leicht verwun
van Gent, Hugo Franz — Frintrop, Oberhausen —
Scholten, Heinrich — Keppeln, Cleve — leicht ver
Göke, Johannes — Bennhausen, Paderborn — leicht
Kambe, Karl — Münster — leicht vermundet.
```

```
belm Subeck — Schnathorst, Minden — schwer verw.
rich Kregel — Naffabel, Kreuzburg — leicht v., b.b. Tr
tav Hauck — Geißelberg, Pirmasens — gefallen.
nislaus Lubeck — Samter — leicht verwundet.
t, Hugo Franz — Frintrop, Oberhausen — leicht verw.
n, Heinrich — Keppeln, Cleve — leicht verwundet.
johannes — Bennhausen, Paderborn — leicht verwundet.
Karl — Münster — leicht verwundet.
```

2nd injury – *Verlustlisten* (List of Injured Soldiers) for 1917, published on 27 May 1918, page 23832

Hugo van Gent – Utffz. (*Unteroffizier*) – 6.5. (date of birth) Frintrop, Essen (place of birth), List Preussen (Prussia) 1147 (Regiment), Government ID FRIROPJO31KL – *leicht verwundet* (wounded lightly)

```
Gentinger [nicht Gantingen]
                    — verwundet 11.
Genrich, Otto — 24. 11. Alt S
van Gent, Hugo, Utffz. — 6. 5.
Gentz, Wilhelm, Gefr., 3. 3. Friedr
Genz, Milli — 6. 7. Hagenow. Gr
```

Hugo and Wilhelmine married relatively late, for the times – he was 31, she was almost 24. There are no real details of his family background, but from the information available, it seems his parents moved to Wesel perhaps to join his uncle, a baker. Two brothers, one nephew, Hugo might have worked in his uncle's bakery, side by side with him. In this photo, he is either one of the seated men at the front.

On the back of the photo, Hugo wrote to Wilhelmine: "In remembrance of our days of being together in Lille (*Zur Erinnerung an die Tage unser Zusammensein in Lille. Von Deinen Hugo Gr. H. Kirchhoff*) Friendship (*Freundschaft*) Until we meet again! (*Auf Wiedersehen!*) Many greetings to xx and Aunt, 1 for Werner, 1 for Little Lotte. One thousand greetings and kisses, Your loyal Hugo / Please Reply (*V Gruesse an Fild und Tante, 1 fuer Werner, 1 fuer Lottchen (?). Tausend Gruesse und Kuesse Dein treuer Hugo / Bitte Antwort*)" Hugo never made it back home to Wesel and his pregnant wife. He died in Halle, Belgium, the last month of WWI (Oct/Nov 1918), during the 100-Day Offensive. This photo he sent to his wife, showing his two comrades, one with an Iron Cross for Bravery, the other with a black-white-red ribbon for 2nd Order Medal of Bravery (tucked into the coat). If she visited him early May, for his 33rd birthday perhaps, they conceived their only daughter at that time, in Lille?

Zur Erinnerung an die Tag...

...Lilli. Dein Hugo

Dr. H. ...

24

...

Schicke dir Geld nach Hause, 1
für ... 1 für ...

Tausend Grüße und Küsse
Dein treuer ...

Lilli ...

Brief recap Franz Hugo Van Gent Family Tree:

Father Antonius Nicolaas Van Gent, born 6 December 1851 in Kleve, Germany (one of 7 children, from first wife) & **Mother** Maria Antonia Louisa Schiffgens, born 1852 in Borbeck, Essen, Germany. Married 12 June 1878, in Borbeck, Essen, Germany

Son Franz Hugo born 6 May 1885 in Frintrop, Essen, Germany

Father's brother (uncle) Johannes Petrus Van Gent, baker, married to (aunt) Maria Petronella Snorn, born 21 June 1843 in Arnhem, Netherlands. Wedded on 1 June 1870, in Arnhem, Netherlands

Son Johannes Andreas Joseph Van Gent, born 6 March 1871-died 6 September 1875

Where Baker Hugo was an only child, his wife Wilhelmine was the last of 7 children (5 boys and 2 girls). Her father is listed as *Gastwirt*, running either a restaurant and/or guest house. He and his wife Elisabeth remained married for 43 and a quarter years. After their wedding day on 26 November 1874, they had one child every 3 years: Max, November 1876; Wilhelm, June 1879; Fritz, March 1881; Paul, September 1884; Emil, August 1887; Johanna (Anna), December 1890 and Wilhelmine, May 1893. In this wedding photo, we see a teenage Wilhelmine (she will turn 14 in one month), standing behind her father. Her brother Max was 17 years older than her. In a time of no mainstream contraception, it is a wonder how Mother Elisabeth timed the pregnancies. Does it mean they only met under the covers every 3 years, she was The Gatekeeper, in a time when pregnancy and childbirth meant a woman always had one foot in the grave?

Wilhelmine's parents: Elisabeth Elgering (24 Feb 1852-20 Dec 1935) and Johann Heinrich Hermann Doehrn (19 July 1847-24 Apr 1918), first photo just married (26 Nov 1874) and second photo 43 ¼ years / 7 children later.

Wesel, 2 April 1907 - Wedding of her oldest brother Max Doehrn to Elly Rautenberg. Wilhelmine was one month short of turning 14, standing behind her father, by his left elbow.

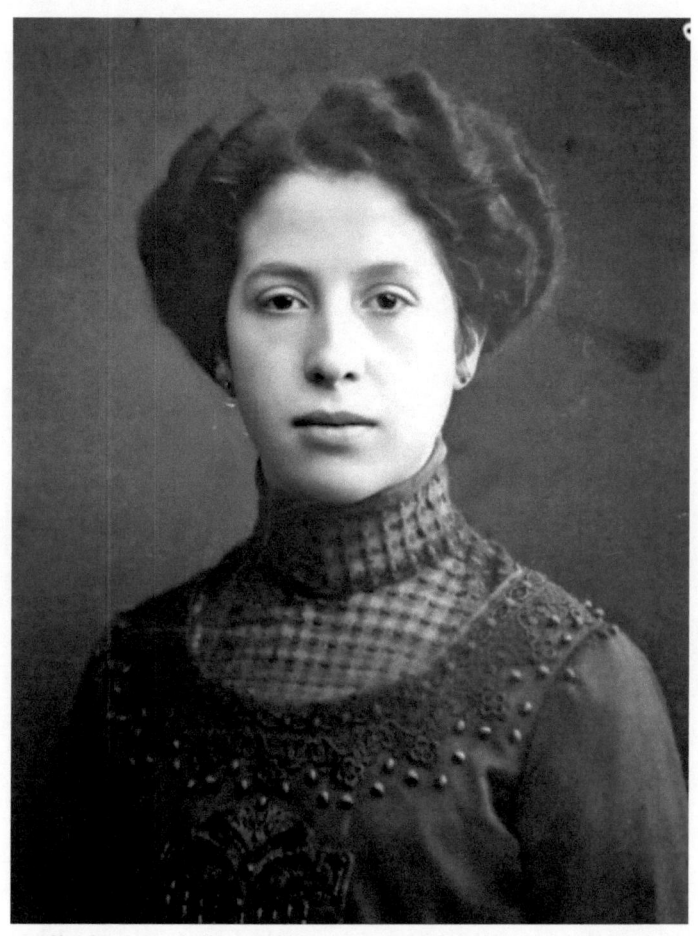

Wilhelmine widowed at 25 years old,.8-months pregnant with only daughter Elisabeth.

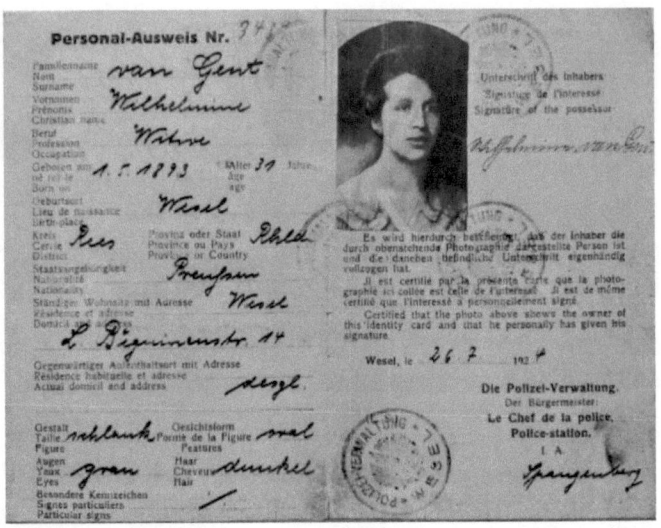

The Doehrn/Van Gent household (Lange Beduinenstrasse 14) was a few blocks away from the Neuenhaus Butcher Shop (Schmidstrasse 28). A few years later, when Wilhelmine's only daughter, Elisabeth Louise was older, did that little girl maybe meet the butcher's son from stopping by there once or twice a week? In 1939, when daughter Elisabeth Louise marries Heinz, was there any fear or worry that history would repeat itself? The war-widow-single mother pattern, a second time around, within 20 years of each other?

When Elisabeth Louise gave birth to her first son, knowing the father was on the Front, discovering in October 1941 that he had died, the Neuenhaus Family remained close to their second grandchild and only remnant of their dead son, and the 22-year old widow.

Window display of Wilhelm Neuenhaus butcher shop, Wesel, 2-3 May 1942 (?) Photos of

Grandmother Emilie, herself born 3 May 1878, one day after her grandson, holding him with love and tenderness. Was it a double-birthday photo, Little Joerg turning 1 and Grandma Neuenhaus turning 64? Grandma Wilhelmine Van Gent also celebrated her birthday around that time, 1 May, she turned 49 in 1942, so it might have been a triple birthday. Quadruple if Grandpa Franz Hugo Van Gent were still alive, he would have turned 57 on 6 May.

Heinz's older brother, Werner, who did come back from the war, with bits of shrapnel in his body, had fathered a little girl, Irmel. Irmel was Joerg's direct cousin, only 2-3 years older. There are photos, Fall and Winter 1941, Year 1 of Baby Joerg, showing his cousin Irmel next to the pram, the butcher shop attendants holding both grandchildren, maybe Ilse and Grandma?

If Liz stayed with Husband#2 for fear he might shoot her if she left, hopefully having her mother with her under the same roof reassured her a little bit; if he tried, he would have to kill them both. Perhaps also the reason why the first few years, Liz only 'lived' with future Husband#2, unwed. They married a few years after living together, circa 1946, when Baby Joerg was 5.

Liz grew up pre-WWII, fatherless. Her mother Wilhelmine decorated Infant Liz with big white bows in her hair, put her in an all-girls' school and always remained at her side. Liz grew up strong and confident, believing in hard work and her capacity for it. Her whole life she slept without pyjamas, to the great distress of her second husband. He found it shocking and was dismayed by this strange habit of hers. Many times he asked her to put on a nightgown, something, for between the sheets, but Liz refused. She was unable to sleep if wearing something, she had to feel that freedom. Even decades later, her son would describe this with wonderment. How dare a woman sleep in the nude?

From 16-19 February to March 1945, Pa's hometown of Wesel was almost entirely destroyed by British bombs. Pa said the only way they knew where the butcher shop had been was from the row of tiles along the floor, all that remained. Cousin Irmel's future husband, Werner, 12 at the time, recalled coming out of the basement bunker once and everything was on fire, even the cow, still standing. He heard the bomb flying over to England, 7 on the dot each evening. Pa, his cousin Ilse, her future husband

Werner and a few thousand others were the survivors of those bombs on Wesel, from 25,000 people in 1939 to 1,900 in 1945. Before the bombing, the Allies dropped leaflets on the town, telling them to evacuate immediately. Most Wesel inhabitants were moved to neighbouring Alsfeld. A decade later, Pa had moved to Kassel, where war rubble collected in a forest south of the city. Nowadays, it is all a beautiful park area, no rubble in sight. Now it is as it was centuries ago, a palace courtyard and hunting ground.

Pa does not recall going hungry in childhood. On one occasion, the family went for a Sunday outing. They could not afford a train or bus, so were grateful when the local logger offered them a ride on his truck. The three kids and mother could sit next to him in the cabin, father sat atop the logs on the back of the truck. They were driven from Alsfeld to Siegen (Germany), into the deep forest. Once there, the logger took them into a small coffee shop, ordered an entire tray of pastries be brought over. 'Pick as many as you want!' he told the kids. Faced with such abundance and assortment, the kids could not even decide on one, regardless two, pastries. It was a wonderful Sunday outing for them.

Afterwards, the family was invited to stay for a few weeks in a logging hut close by. Pa, his brother and sister roamed the woods around the cabin, built dams in the rivulet below, piling pebbles up, wading barefoot up to their ankles. Pa polished the family's shoes, letting the freshly-waxed shoes dry on the terrace. It was a grand holiday.

Ma's eating habits were forged during those many years of deprivation. She tried her first banana when she was 12, sugar was a once-in-a-week highlight, a teaspoon dissolved in a glass of water for a Saturday Treat. When Ma's mother was in her 8th month of pregnancy, she was put on a train with dozens of other women and children, to be evacuated from Vienna, which was being bombed by Allies. The trains brought them to the countryside, farms took them up, they worked as farmhands in exchange for safe room and board.

In Schaerding, where Oma arrived, she worked for an aged farming couple. She delivered Friedi and was hospitalised thereafter for an infection of the milk ducts. She had breastfed Ma, the infected milk caused the baby's body to be covered in pustules. Oma was kept in hospital, they slit her breasts open on either side to drain out the pus and infected milk. Ma, tiny newborn, was almost abandoned in the farmhouse, she screamed for hours, they say it was a miracle she survived. She had a scar on her arm thereafter, of where they had cut open a pustule, to drain it. Ma was born with a fighting spirit, making her a formidable force if anyone crossed or stood in her way. The older farming couple offered young new mother Anita half a pig in exchange for the baby girl, 'You are young, you will still bear many children, we have no one to help us or leave the farm to.' Anita kept her baby girl.

SISTERS REUNITED

Anita knew how difficult and lonely life could be. When she was 5, her mother died. Her father, unable to care for her and her younger sister, Gisi (Gisela), 3, brought both children to a care home. There they were adopted separately, Gisi by an aunt and Anita by a widow, growing up apart until they met again for Anita's wedding, 20 years later. Their father, forbidden to visit his daughters by over-protective adoptive families, probably committed suicide by drowning himself in the Danube, widowed and childless, in despair.

Here is one of the first photos of younger sister Gisi with her "new" adoptive family. The grandmother sitting in the polka dot dress instructed her daughter's husband to go to the care home and bring home one of the girls. Apparently the couple chose Gisi because of her light blue eyes, unlike her older sister Anitas' very black eyes. (approx date of photo is 1927). Next photo, Gisi at her Confirmation, aged +-6 yrs old, 1923-4.

44

Here we see 2 sisters in their adoptive families – a teenage Gisi (1930-32?) and center stage with distant paternal relatives; Anita (maybe 13-4, 1925-6), with Tante Mina & Dog Pinky. These two young girls became the light and hope of their adoptive parents.

Below, their reunion more than 15 years later, for Anita's wedding, on 9 September 1936 in Dornbach (leafy suburb of Vienna, Austria).

Anita was 23 (almost 24, born 6 November 1912), Gisi just turned 19 (born 24 May 1917), two sisters reunited, never to be parted again.

ANITA'S DAUGHTER FRIEDI BREAKS FREE

Years later, Ma had tonsillitis and the doctors advised to remove them. The anaesthetic wore off during the operation and 12-year-old Friedi heard, saw and felt everything, saw blood everywhere. The nuns holding her down during the surgery told her to stop screaming when she reacted in fright. 'Quiet, girl, quiet! No screaming, stay still!' Her fighting spirit was almost paralysed by her father's abuse, both verbal and physical. Whatever pushed Franz to be so hard on his eldest daughter – his war trauma, his being the youngest spoiled son, his alcoholism – is no justification for his mistreatment of Friedi. Punishing her by making her kneel in the corner with her face to the wall, for hours, his heavy hand hitting her time and time again. When Friedi finished the girls' cooking and sewing school at 16, she took the first opportunity to get as far away from her father as possible, hatred, anger and loathing propelling her all the way to Versailles, France, where she worked as an *au paire* for a family with 4 children. Friedi never forgave her father, did not attend his or her mother's funeral, had only venom for any memory of him. Her mother and grandmother had watched helplessly as he beat her, both crying, neither of them intervening, only adding more hatred to Friedi's fighting spirit. Not only was her father a stranger to her, her mother and grandmother as well, if they would not stand up to him. Friedi never felt more alone, helpless and betrayed as then.

If Ma felt betrayed by her parents, she loved her paternal grandmother, Marie Danzinger. Marie was Handsome Alexander's (*Schoener Alex*) second wife, his first wife having died during childbirth, mother and baby both dead. The bedsheets had an embroidered 'MP' on them, Maria Peininger. Handsome Alexander kept the sheets from that first dowry and found himself Marie Danzinger. Although they had the same last name, they were not related. To marry, they had to request permission all the way up to the bishop, who granted it. Marie was shy and did not consider herself attractive, was thus intimidated at being chosen by Handsome Alexander to be his wife. She slept on the sheets of the dead first wife and bore 3 sons, outliving Handsome Alex after his death of typhus during WWII. There would have been 2 girls as well, born after the 3 boys, but they died, at 3-months old and the other right after childbirth. Both baby girls were born blue (probably Rhesus-factor).

Marie had a sister, Agnes and brother Franz. Agnes was a beauty, working as housemaid in larger residences across the countryside by Waidhofen, Austria. The patron of one such a residence raped her, she bore an illegitimate son. When she married Karl Ricker in Vienna years later, her husband made that bastard son eat his meals under the dining table, as punishment for his embarrassing origin. Fortunately, this son did not end up a killer or psycho, he left the house as soon as he could and lived his own life joyfully. Agnes' grandson became known as Fat Karli, for his eating habits. It was expected that Fat Karli would one day marry his second-cousin Maria. When she rejected him, icy silence descended on the family. This had occurred earlier, Agnes criticised Handsome Alex and Marie did not forgive her, the sisters did not speak for 12 years.

After the war and widowhood, sister Agnes and Marie reconciled, sitting together in Marie's kitchen, talking, while 3 grandchildren bounded around the tiny apartment. Agnes' grandson Karli would be jumping around with the 2 sisters, so wildly, they broke Agnes' walking stick in two. In the corner was an *Inrusa-Bett* (foldable bed with a metal frame), for the daytime *Bettgeher*, a homeless worker who paid rent to sleep in the bed. Marie had a cat, the cat jumped up onto the shelf and peed on the Xmas chocolates, hidden away. Once a travelling salesman came to sell a hardcover cookbook to Marie and daughter-in-law Anita. When son Franz came home and saw they had bought this expensive book, he yelled at both women for falling in on the salesman's pitch.

On another occasion, Franz promised to come home with a turkey. On the way home, he stopped in a bar to meet his pals. When he came home, the bundle he laid on the table was his dirty shirt, covered in vomit. Franz's wartime years left him more insufferable than ever.

Marie also had a little brother, Georgie. When they were all children, Georgie was sent with a few cents to the bakery, to pick up some bread for dinner. He spent the money on sweets instead, ate them, was so afraid and worried as to the scolding he would get, he wandered away from the path home. He would hide out in the forest for a while, then go back home, when they would forget his misdemeanour. In the darkness, he wandered into the moors, could not swim. When they went looking for him, all they found was his cap floating on the surface, poor little Georgie had drowned in the marshes, alone, filled with sugar and guilt. Marie would tell her granddaughters this story and weep, the heartbreak and loss still hurt after all those decades.

Marie had 3 second-nieces, sisters Johanna, Polderl and Anna. Polderl was engaged to German soldier Schlueter, on assignment in Austria. Overheated from some exercise, he jumped into an icy river and died of a heart attack, leaving his pregnant Polderl a widow. Her mother made her marry the dead soldier, so that the baby would not be illegitimate. Polderl, widow and single mother of Werner, never remarried.

After the war, only 2 of Marie's 3 sons came back. The eldest, most like his father, tall and handsome, was declared Missing In Action, lost in the Battle of Stalingrad. Mother Marie and Alex Jr.'s wife, Poldi, waited their whole life for him, ever hopeful that he was only Missing and not Dead. It was in vain, Alex Jr. never came back. Poldi bossed her sister and son around, hiring her sister to clean the apartment and seating her son at a desk in front of hers in the office. She was the boss in the office, always keeping an eye on her youngest son, Klemens. Unable to extricate himself from her commandeering, Klemens shrunk into a hen-pecked shell and died at 65, in an old-age home, never having learned to dress and feed himself, never going on a date, never meeting a girl, remaining forever that little boy. In his leather briefcase, he carried x-rated magazines around, his only escape from his mother's grasp.

Middle son Fritz came back from the Northern Front, followed by a beautiful lover. Adele sung songs in Estonian, knit beautiful gloves, cooked and cleaned with smooth efficiency. Although Fritz had left a wife and son in Vienna, during the war lines blurred, life was short, one lived for the day. Vienna wife Emmi had herself interned in a hospital for those with respiratory ailments, in the countryside, to breathe fresh mountain air. Fritz moved between his first married apartment and the second acquired one. Lunchtime and laundry with Adele, nights at home with Emmi and son Helmut.

When Helmut turned 20, he fell in love with a seamstress. His father was incensed, he had not paid for his son's engineering studies to see him marrying down, there were better prospects.

When father and son disagreed and butted heads on the new girlfriend, Helmut yelled, 'You have no right to tell me who to date, you a married man with another woman on the side!' That was the break, father and son went separate ways, each with their woman of choice. In death, Fritz lay in his tomb with both his women, official wife Emmi and common law wife Adele, all 3 together in death as they had been in life.

From his childhood, Pa appreciated Americans and that is why he put his 3 daughters into the American School in Mexico City, and not the German School. When Pa first went to 'America' in 1967, it was with a 6-month visa for Montreal. He and another Austrian-German couple were going to work in America for 6 months during Expo 67. It was the time of Prime Minister Trudeau (father) dating starlets, Liz & Richard had married in Montreal 3 years earlier, glam & glitz. Also, if Pa went to Montreal, there was no draft for the Vietnam War, which was still an issue in the USA.

In 1969, Pa met Ma. She was in Montreal waiting for her Austrian confectionery baker boyfriend to come back from his 2-month work stint in New York City. She had been following Guenther Karner around Europe and the UK for the past 6 years, she was in love. She was not granted a visa to the USA, so waited for Guenther to come back. One day he called from NYC and said, 'Friedl, I am not coming back, I met someone else, German Christl.' Ma was shattered, she thought she would die. She was preparing to fly back home to Vienna, her 6-month visa for Canada would run out soon. Then she went to a *Fasching* (Carnival) Party and met Pa. After one year of dating, she got pregnant. December 1970 Boxing Day first daughter came along, in the Royal Victoria Hospital on Mount-Royal. May 1973 second daughter came along. A few months later, move to Vancouver, British Columbia. 1976 move to Mexico City, 1979 third daughter was born there.

Their WWII memories did not come out until their daughters were in their 20s. First Daughter bothered the parents with questions, before becoming a teen, 'Did you have many boyfriends before Pa, Ma?' or 'When you were growing up, did you have a bicycle?' and other childish worries. They never answered, always just said, 'No no, that was long ago.' Then slowly stories started coming out. Last Summer we were playing cards and somehow we got to Pa's delicate stomach and how he threw up a whole glass of cold milk on one of their first dates in a Cape Cod restaurant. Pa said, 'Yes, your mother trapped me! She got pregnant and that was it, I was trapped!' Even so, marriage was a law not to be broken, you stayed with it, it was for life. They were both *Kriegskinder* (children of the war) who had grown up among the rubble and knew how short life could be, how sparse, no abundance, so many deprivations, no time or space for sentimentality.

Pa despaired over his eldest daughter, she did not stick with anything, had no perseverance. It took her many decades to realise that sometimes decisions or choices cannot be undone or redone, there is no path back to do it another way or say something different. Even if she were to think, 'Oh, I will only do this quickly for now, then I will adjust,' or 'Oh, I will go there but only for a short time, check it out, if it does not work, I will come back.' Often there was no do-over or going back. That was life, a few steps in a certain direction might be irreversible, permanent, that was it, you had to live with it, final. It meant loss, farewell, not holding on too much, not putting everything on hold for that one person or goal, somehow juggling it all at the same time, improvising, letting some things go by the wayside. Taking it on the chin, giving the other cheek, his eldest was not good at that. The younger generation were just too weak and coddled.

Neighbour Irmgard remembers the death and poverty she saw growing up during WWII. She was one of 5 children. When the last infant got sick, her parents brought her to the hospital. The doctor said, 'Sorry, we have nothing, not even cotton, there is nothing we can do, leave her lying there next to the windowsill, you can pick up the body tomorrow.' The children had only one pair of shoes each, in Winter feet were permanently cold and wet, sinking in the snow, no chance to let shoes dry for a day or two. Clothing was mended and remended, passed from one child to the next. Children were not allowed to speak when seated at the table, obedience was everything.

Seventy-five years later, Irmgard owned a huge collection of crèches, filling 3 boxes for storage during the year. At Christmas, she unwrapped each one and placed them on every surface in her house. They were from all over the world, made from all kinds of materials – rock, shells, corn husks, cork, glass, clay. Although she was widowed after 30 years of marriage and had no children, she collected and displayed these nativity scenes almost every December. Perhaps she was always searching for that infant sibling she lost so cruelly after the war.

Cousin Hildegard was malnourished and when the war ended in 1945, was sent to relatives to be fed and fattened up. The relatives had a butcher shop and sold a few dried goods on the side. Hildegard, age 5, was tasked with preparing small amounts of sugar and flour for sale. She weighed 100 grams of sugar, 250 grams of flour, packed it away neatly in paper bags. She worked neatly and carefully, garnering admiring comments and compliments from her relatives. What a wonderful time that had been, she had a task to do and was rewarded for doing it well. Numbers, scales, small packages, lined up on the shelf, ready for tomorrow's shoppers. Life could be nice, even if there was war and its ravages. There was hope.

March 2020

ITALIAN ZING

The tiny Italian bar hung onto the last end of the busy market, almost hidden away in the next block. Barely 8 seats inside, pressed up against a wooden board along the window, acting as table surface. "Rosmarino" was not a place to sit, eat and talk for hours. It was to grab a quick cup of coffee or glass of *prosecco*, a bite of croissant or cheese, say a quick hello to charming Aristide, filling orders, or his Austrian boss Frau Rauch.

Customers flocked to this tiny corner of Italy in the middle of the square, trying to forget the grey Winter, fog and cloudy days, melting into black afternoons at 4pm. Any Southern warmth was soaked up eagerly, even if it was only a few minutes squeezed into an Italian deli. That wonderful Italian zing, highly personified by Aristide, pulled clients in like a magnet. He smiled, chit-chatted, charmed, made everyone leave feeling happy and a bit buzzed, in a good way.

Then came Corona, the world stood still. When shops and restaurants slowly reopened 2 years later, there was no more Aristide. Apparently he was trying his luck in New York, of course, far more exciting than being stuck in that tiny bar. Certainly a loss for us guests, no more eye candy to take in from afar, while biting into a salty olive and washing it down with some bubbly. So many things cut, interrupted, stopped by Corona, the Before Corona and After Corona life.

July 2021

WORK OR SEX

The rivalry between the two women had started when Younger Newer seduced the boss and he got a heart attack. Older Straighter had put up with YN coming in, clawing accounts and work away from her, she who had kept the office afloat the past 8 years, navigating it through the messy divorce, Wife Exit from the Office & Personal Life, OS answered the phone, paid the bills, showed up at her desk when no one else did. After 8 years of sacrifice, YN waltzed in, pulled work her way, took Boss to bed and then when she realised, 'Oh dear, I do love my husband and kids after all, I do love my country house and the garden, I cannot leave them for Boss and City Life,' again it was OS who kept the office going and bills paid, while Boss tried to recover from the Sex Mess and his heart attack. YN had to decide, if she was to keep working, she had to keep Boss alive, so no sex games with him. His heart had not been able to do it all, Work & Sex in the office, not at 53 anymore, anyway. A few years ago, perhaps, but now the body was weaker, longer recovery time.

OS's contempt of YN was justified, even if it was the age-old story of Woman coming into Male Office Turf and bedding the Boss. Women's rivalry played out not against each other, but via the Male Bosses.

At the jewellers, decades ago, it had been the same. Brunette managed the store for Tall Boss, then Black-Hair Beauty elbowed her way in and convinced TB to open a second store, in the suburbs. Great set-up for Tall Boss, two women fighting over him, managing his jewellery stores, bringing him physical and material profits, win-win-win. His mother supervised both stores, leaving him enough leeway to bed other women, there were so many coming his way, all wanted to breathe Jewellery Store Air and be driven around in his Corvettes. After years of these antics, Mother, Brunette and Black-Hair Beauty contented themselves with only managing his stores, keeping their fingers and attention away from his increasingly voluminous personal conquests. His funeral was organised by Latest Capture, no one liked or knew her, she came preaching how to eat and live healthy, last-ditch effort to save his ailing health. When Triumvirate of Senior Women did not let her into the business, she moved on and quickly found the next Male Case to Heal.

Indeed, Cat-Fights amongst Women after one of them had bedded The Boss were quite deadly.

I DO NOT WANT TO DIE ALONE

Or do I? Manolo and Manolin had died alone, found by their cleaning ladies, one in Malaga, the other in Mallorca. I had last seen Manolo having a late-night pizza and red wine in Pizza Riva. Since they had removed part of his tongue and mouth tissue due to cancer from heavy smoking, his body remained rail-thin, no matter how much he ate, he never regained enough weight to a healthy level. I greeted him and he continued eating hungrily, was it his only meal that day? After a few weeks in the city, he flew off to the coast, sea and sun. Three weeks there, he had packed and was getting ready to board the plane back to mainland the next day. When did the heart attack happen, how did he end up lying on his kitchen floor? The cleaning lady only called the police, not venturing any closer to the body. Manolin had been similar, only he was on his living room floor, a life-long smoker and drinker. It was incredible in itself that both these men had made it to late-60s at all. When their friends spoke of their death, they said, 'They were alone at home,' as if it were a disease or a virus.

The two women anaesthesiologists had chosen death on their own terms, each giving herself the proper dose. They would know, it was their profession, career, they had been setting anaesthetic doses for surgery during medical school and then in hospitals. The younger one, in her late 50s, had cleaned out her locker in the hospital, written out a clear will and shot herself the lethal dose at home. It was 6 months after her husband had gone down in a plane accident, 5 urologists on board on their way to a conference. She and her husband had met during med school, shared the villa with his mother, their daughter happily married. She could not imagine life without him, so she joined him in death as she had joined him during life. The second anaesthesiologist was in her 80s, looking back on an extensive career which covered teaching, travelling, conferences, books. When she realised she was starting to forget words, an early sign of dementia, she gave herself the lethal dose, ensuring it was the right amount to send her off to sleep permanently. These two women had decided to die alone.

Will we greet death when it is time, or will we wait for it to surprise us?

August 2019

NOTARY CUTHBERT

No one could accuse Notary Cuthbert of leading a dissipated life, '*una vida disipada.*' Indeed, if anything, Notary Cuthbert led a most exemplary life, balanced, routine, of careful action, patiently building up his client base, checking his bank account every few days, keeping mental checks and balances. Shopping in the luxury Big City mall was only allowed every few months, when the bank account permitted, no purchases on credit, that would be careless. His fingernails were trimmed to thin slivers of moon, clean, even.

For all the care and attention Notary Cuthbert put into his appearance and office, there was the extreme debauchery and excesses of one of his main clients to cover. Fumann was the single son of a local politician, doted upon by an old-school patriarch. When the Over-Father was not indulging his latest mistresses, he was meeting Notary Cuthbert every Friday on the golf course. During those 18-holes, they would discuss business, neglected properties to be picked up, ownership writs to be transferred, government offices to be oiled. That property empire would one day go to Fumann, the Golden Son. Growing up with such abundance, knowing the land was his, Fumann embarked on all kinds of foolish enterprises – a boxing stint, a city councillor candidacy – while inhaling copious amounts of hallucinogenic and stimulating drugs. Fumann pushed his body to the edge, until he lay connected to tubes on a hospital bed in his father's house at Relatively Young Age 45. Death swayed over him.

Where Notary Cuthbert had a moderate lunch every afternoon between 2 and 4pm, living every day like clockwork, Fumann had crisscrossed the country in his private helicopter, drank all bars dry, left all indiscreet nightclubs with dozens of women, blurring day and night, work and play. Fumann could do anything, the money-well never dried out, his Patriarch had worked his whole life to fill that safe. So it was that Notary Cuthbert outlived Patriarch's son by a good many decades, thanks to his ascetic lifestyle and cautious moves. With scorn he had stamped Fumann's life Lost and Wasted.

August 2019

GONE SUDDENLY

Walter Kramer grew up knowing he would follow in his father's footsteps and become a furrier as well. His father's shop was in a four-block area covered by 84 furrier shops, spoiling clients with choice. Potential clients would go from shop to shop, comparing wares and prices. After learning the trade, he worked beside his father, sewing furs into coats ordered by the dozen by a large retail chain. To live out his creativity, he took up painting and joined the Furrier Guild, actively recruiting younger furriers, sitting on the test panel, collecting boxes filled with papers and photos of the 573 years of guild activity. His store flourished, he could divide his time between a city apartment and a country house with garden.

At 61, he decided it was enough, one more year of working and then he would close the shop, enjoy a comfortable retirement. He went on a strict diet, became rail thin and felt the best he had felt in years. April he complained of migraines, went to a few doctors, got a few prescriptions, was told it was fatigue, just a few symptoms of ageing. July he was on the panel testing new joiners to the Furrier Guild. As he asked a question of the candidate, the answer came and Mr Kramer had no answer, could not elaborate or evaluate the answer. 'How was this certain fur identified?' he had asked. When the answer came, he had forgotten the question and could not judge the reply. The panel agreed to break until the next day, 'Rest up a bit, Walter, we'll continue tomorrow, must be the extreme heat.'

A few days later, Walter Kramer was in hospital with other symptoms. An inoperable aggressive brain tumour was found, it grew so quickly and destroyed him within weeks, he never left the hospital. Three weeks later, Walter Kramer died, close to the desired retirement of his 62nd year of life. His tall, thin figure no longer unlocked the security gate from his shop every morning, point 8, punching in the security code for his alarm. Walking elegantly with an umbrella, bowing and greeting, always the polite gentleman, from one moment to the next he was gone. Summer began, Summer ended, Walter Kramer left with it. No farewell, no chance to wish the best, no time to enjoy retirement. Just like that, finger-snap, gone. Only his last name, KRAMER, was left written on the doorbell names list.

September 2019

BREAD CRUNCH

The breakfast routine was the same every day. Unlock office door, deposit bag on desk, go to supermarket for fresh bread, butter and cheese.

Back in the office kitchen, lean on bread bun in paper bag with full body weight, crunch the crust down with both hands to soften it, cut bun in half, spread both halves with butter, cover with thick slabs of smelly cheese, boil water for 1 litre of green tea, drag everything to the desk, sit in front of screen, bite into bread whilst answering the first mails and calls.

The weight on the bread bun was the deciding factor, that crust had to be flattened before the day started, precursor to flattening all other things and people that day.

September 2019

STUFFING ENVELOPES

She had taken the job to earn a bit of cash and inhale some Downtown Elegant Art Gallery Air. 'You applied for the assistant job but we need some envelope stuffers today, can you come?' an Eastern European voice asked on the phone. A few hours later, she sat at a table with a Muslim girl, a deaf girl and a blonde doll-lookalike, the four of them stuffing 2,000 envelopes with an auction flyer. The gallery owner, well into his 80s, ranted and raged across the beautiful parquet floor, 'Pick up those envelopes! Sort those! Empty the dust bin! Label these with the district number!' His barking voice echoed across the elegant windows and displays.

Coming in the door, Foreign Assistant greeted her. 'Prada, is that Prada?' she asked.

'No, just the cheapie scent at the pharmacy cash register, the one on special for 7 Euros,' Stuffer explained.

Prada?! If she could afford a Prada perfume, would she be here on a Tuesday afternoon stuffing envelopes for a bit of cash?! After intensive envelope-stuffing for 3 and a half hours, she had spent the 42 Euros on a theatre ticket (13 Euros), a cafe latte (4 Euros) and a few supermarket visits. Had the cash gone to an expensive perfume bottle, it would have been just enough for a tiny bottle, 3 spritzes of scent, faded after a day on the go, definitely not a good investment. So no, she was not wearing Prada perfume.

October 2019

SNIP SNIP

All three men had vasectomies in their late 40s. They had kids, were on to their second wife maybe, had closed shop for any further procreation. Their manhood was not threatened by those two little snips. One wanted to ensure his wife did not end up pregnant with Baby #3, she wanted half a dozen if possible, but he was already content with 3. In another case, Wife #2 also wanted half a dozen kids, to stay home, charge everything to the credit card, hire a cleaning lady and enjoy life between beauty salon and dropping the kids off at school. Husband felt the weighty stone of decades working to pay for her and their children's bills, panicked and secretly went for a vasectomy, not informing her of his decision.

September 2019

I AM

the baby crawling through long Summer grass on Mount Royal in 1971.

the girl on a tricycle, next to the lilac bush and crooked peach tree in the corner of the Vancouver backyard.

the girl on a bicycle in Chapultepec Park (Mexico City), losing her first ring, with a large blue stone, from Oma.

the girl crashing along the cement sidewalk on Buenos Aires Street (1980, Guadalajara, Jalisco), metal rollerskates flying, watching helplessly as her sister falls and chips her top front tooth.

sitting in the front seat of the school bus, looking up to the rearview mirror, seeing herself next to her sister, both of us dishevelled, hungry and tired, only wanting to get home. We look so different, yet the same. (1979)

the girl bounding about in ballet and gymnastics, ice-skating, on roller coasters in amusement parks.

the girl pining for so many boys who would not even take notice of her, taking refuge in the library.

reading and loving heroines in Jane Austen, Charlotte Bronte and rose-coloured Barbara

Cartland novels, dreaming of The Prince Who Will Come And Sweep Her Off Her Feet.

the stubborn teenager butting heads with her parents on everything from clothing, friends, to going out on Friday night.

the twentysomething struggling with weight, college and being on her own in a world of grown-ups.

the thirtysomething going from job to job to job, thinking each time, 'I hope this one holds.'

the fortysomething facing health scares and white hair after too many office politics attacks.

the cook, cleaning lady, masseuse, open ear, seamstress, the one who picks it all up.

the free woman realising there is no prince, and it is better that way, freedom is a greater way of life.

November 2019

LOST SISTERS

Is it not odd that my two close friends lost sisters as well? In their younger years, unexpectedly, one from illness, the other from a car accident, leaving them stunned and bereft, as we were.

Decades later, we name our lost sisters' names and feel the ache as acutely as then, that hole, that loss, that physical punch in the gut. We understand each other beyond words, our tragedies unite us. We all miss the sister we lost.

November 2019

CELL MEMORY

The purpose of the body is to translate outer sensations to micro-electric charges, transmitted to our cells. These cells will then live on in other forms of matter, carrying that electric memory with it, passing on that charge to whichever living element it is in next. So we must be sure to ensure positive charges, positive memories and experiences, for our positive cells will then transmit that message, Morse code, to its next vessel – plant, animal or human.

November 2019

PACEMAKER 1

A white donkey was adopted for the baroque castle petting zoo. Giving it a new home and new family would ensure this rare breeds' genetic survival, in case any in-breeding or ill fortune should befall the other white donkey family.

A few weeks after moving the white donkey to its new rural castle, veterinarians determined the poor animal had a weak, malfunctioning heart, he was on the edge of death. Quickly heart doctors from the country's best hospital were called in, they performed surgery on the noble animal and put in a heart pacemaker. This great generosity to a lowly beast was written about in all newspapers, all headlines.

Unfortunately, death did not stay far and came back too soon. Humans were unaware that the pacemaker in the donkey would beat more, spending the battery faster than in humans. One morning, caretakers found the white donkey still asleep in his box. He had fallen asleep, the pacemaker battery had beat itself out, no more beating heart for the rare white donkey.

December 2019

PACEMAKER 2

The body was to be cremated. The grieving widow signed all papers in the hospital, drowning in tears, exhausted by sadness and countless sleepless nights, at her husband's hospital bed. The body was sent to the morgue, rolled into the cremation furnace. Suddenly a huge explosion tore the furnace apart, damaging the morgue as well. What had been in that casket, they wondered?

Upon in-depth inquiries, it was determined that the husband's pacemaker had blown up in the furnace, causing such extensive flames that the widow was sent an additional bill for thousands of Euros of repairs. Since then, many forms must be signed before cremation, all pacemakers must be removed from the body before sending it to the morgue. If not all forms are sent, no cremation, since no morgue wants to be left with costs to rebuild itself.

December 2019

WOMAN AMAZON

Risa does not like yellow toilet paper, she prefers the one with lilac designs. She rides her bicycle to work, has a large tattoo on her left arm, only wants to work with women and has angular handwriting with large flourishes and long lines. Her curls are cut to a short bob, so that she seems an impersonation of Virginia Woolf or Clara Bow from the 20s. Her lunches are steamed vegetables with a bit of dressing, healthy and no-frills. Her cigarette breaks on the office balcony coincide with long phone conversations or prickly workplace politics needing ironing out. When she was told once that throwing cigarette butts into the trash can smelled up the whole kitchen, Risa was angered and carried this criticism of her habit around for days and weeks, letting it fester and bubble inside of her. The girl who had dared the critical comment was promptly fired after one month on the job.

Risa could afford to get worked up about these tiny unimportant details, she was the owners' lover and manager. Owner Sylvia could take off one week each month to a beach or island, knowing Risa would keep things moving. Sylvia could even sustain her tiny little coke habit, knowing Risa's sturdy shoulders would carry it all, would juggle the girls in their account jobs, would be on the phone to clients, would sweet-talk potential clients and moody creatives. Risa was even strict and bossy with Sylvia's dog, commanding it to sit, walk beside her or stop jumping around. Dog was dog, not a personality or character to be spoiled.

When Sylvia came back from her latest one-week island escape, Risa said nothing of the visible excess signs. Sylvia's face was burnt to a deep crisp blackness, far beyond any healthy suntanning. Two or three spots had remained entirely baby pink or white, a few neck wrinkles and that round patch by the left nostril, as big as a dollar coin. How had that happened, had Sylvia spread her suntan oil or ineffective blocker so unevenly? Or was it the left nostril used for snorting that wonderful white sugar dust which quelled Sylvia's appetite, so she felt energised for hours and needed no food? The perfect combination, because Sylvia needed to sell properties, pitch new clients, make calls to past customers, remind them she was there. After those high-performance tasks, she had a small natural yogurt, keeping her trim figure and fitting into her skin-tight jeans. Appearances mattered, if Sylvia looked like a million bucks, she would eventually earn them too.

Risa also gave Sylvia all the loose rein for sexual grazing. Sylvia had just chucked Marriage#2, had a boy toy 10 years younger than her, marathon runner and very married Steven. Only Steven had access to Sylvia's calendar, but Sylvia's voracious appetite was not satisfied with this young buck. For a bit more spice and variety, there was Risa, Reliable Risa, running her office and always there for a drink after work, a few glasses of prosecco in the office and then a bit more. Where Risa was only a one-woman partner, she turned a blind eye to Sylvia's all-engulfing appetite and indulged her, even delivering a few young innocent lambs for sacrifice in the form of office receptionists. If the receptionist wanted to keep her job, she had to intuitively know she was there to be Sylvia's new toy and distraction. Risa lured them in with the promise of work and a salary, Sylvia reeled them on to be lunch on her plate. Great teamwork for Risa and Sylvia.

February 2020

MATHS PANIC

She could still see that white paper in front of her, with rows and rows of equations, plus, minus, divisions, multiplications. The clock was ticking, around her all other classmates were quickly and furiously filling in answers with pencils waving frantically. She felt trapped, as if tied to her chair and desk, staring intently at the paper but seeing nothing, understanding nothing, fearing the moment the teacher would say, 'Time's up, pencils down!' and walk up and down the aisles, collecting the weekly math quiz. Those equations, like little black ants on the paper, caused her nightmares.

The teacher had spoken to her mother, 'she has to relax a little, not take it so earnestly, then she will do just fine.' Ma did not know how to translate this, tried practicing with me at home. Of course then it always went well, quick and easy. It was only in the classroom, when the long hand on the clock tick tick ticked too fast and she could never fill in all the answers until the bottom of the page. She sat, pencil poised over paper, feeling as if she were drowning, anxiety building up, misery seeping in, tears on the edge, frustration and anger welling up inside her. There it was, that agony, all over again, she thought, helpless. Once that took hold of her, she might as well crumple up the paper and run from the classroom, it was no use, she would never get those darned equations. Those little black ants would chase her the whole school year.

Years later, eleven years to be exact, that same anxiety came back to haunt her during the first university term, exam time, mid-terms. Three-hour tests, seated in one of 20 rows of desks in a huge gym, the clock ticking, observers pacing the aisles, making sure there was no cheating going on. Her mind went blank, she reread test questions 10, 20 times and could not come up with any logical reply, no number of paragraphs to fill the pages of the test booklet, no dates, years, definitions, quotes, examples of whatever philosophical concept she should have learned in that first semester. The weeks and days leading up to exams were torture, she drowned her distress by eating inordinate amounts of cookies, muffins, chocolate, easily joining the Club of Freshman 40 (40 pounds gained in 1st-year university). It took her the entire last two years at university to lose that extra weight, diets, gym visits, group therapy sessions, all that to undo the nerves and anxiety from that first year.

Only one more time after university was there that dreaded Exam Anxiety. Redoing her driving license from one country to another required a new written and practical exam. The written exam lasted one hour, questions were multiple choice, all done on a computer. No practical exam without passing the written one. She was supposed to study for it evenings and weekends. After 5 years of this, she registered for the test and paid the required EUR 100. After failing, she could try again within the same year. Luckily, this time she did not binge or gorge on food, diverting her stress and anxiety into gym visits instead. She did eventually pass the test and got her driver's license reissued in the new country, even without any weight gain. If she could avoid it, she would never need to do any other exams, ever.

April 2012

WET WITH SWEAT AND RAIN

The embossed card had the golden crest of an official embassy invitation and the name in beautiful, swirling calligraphy. Elegant event in a palace downtown, during lunch. A few other colleagues were invited, they decided to carpool to get there. Wearing office garb, they arrived at the downtown palace as heavy rain came down. No parking was to be found. They drove into a nearby garage, no space, got stuck, lost a quarter of an hour manoeuvering back and forth. Out under the rain again, they circled a few blocks and finally found a spot. Car Owner had no parking permit or stub to stay for 2 hours, so she volunteered to run to the closest tobacconist and buy a parking stub. The rain pelted down. They were late. She rushed to the tobacconist and back. Parking stub in place, well-displayed in the front window, they ran into the palace as more buckets of rain came down. In a large hall, men in suits and uniforms gave long speeches. The guests were soaked from the rain and sweat, from rushing to get there. There were no seats, standing for so long made all weary. After a few more dull addresses to the crowd, lunch was announced, 'The Embassy invites you to open the buffet.'

Everyone rushed down, expecting a nice, warm meal. Instead, they were greeted by sparse tables, no chairs or other seating possibilities and a grand buffet offering slaw, sausages and a few slices of dark bread. Beer or wine were available, but waiting staff barely circulated and it was a challenge to obtain a beverage. After swallowing down a bit of these meagre offerings, the guests went back to their offices, back to work, bedraggled, wet, sweaty, bored by the dull speeches, still hungry. It had all started so nicely, sounded so nicely, then ended up being simply a wet, grey afternoon.   Summer 2017

RECEPTIONIST

Tell me who your receptionist is and I will tell you who you are.

Is she a fake blonde ditz or a serious brunette? Is her skirt too tight to walk in, most of her anatomy visible, leaving little to the imagination? Is she every man's fantasy at night in bed with them? The dry lawyers want to show their Dominican bombshell is really cool, as they really are. No, they are not a bunch of nerds who had their nose in books for years and now make so much money, they can afford to pay for a doll out front.

Is she at least 40 years younger than the white-haired boss, whose wife does the hiring and he nixes each decent candidate in favour of the nubile ones? The wife filters new recruits, sends in the married, bookish ones, husband wants eye candy out front and flouncing around his table, so he goes for semi-naked teenage daughter of friends, looking for a little extra cash on the side while she studies.

Is she an older model, staid, motherly, no risk of attraction, no distraction for eye or mind, reliable, matronly, serving coffee from years of servitude and resignation? Is she the in-between model, older but wearing rebellious sneakers, high-tops, to signal, 'I am still cool, I am trapped in this job but move around nimbly and can flaunt the dress code, because I have been here long enough and am now allowed some liberties?'

It is the few who go for an open, friendly face, breaking that cliche, taking a receptionist who means business and dresses the part. Where have the good ones gone?

April 2020

DOG PARK SOCIAL

When entering the Dog Park, it is best to walk up and down the perimeter a few times, absorbed in one's own thoughts. Do not greet other dog owners or dogs. Appear aloof. If the dogs play together, snarl and chase each other, continue pretending this is too dull and routine to be of any interest. Do not ask the names of other dogs, do not comment on how cute, how funny, how beautiful their dog is. Do not ask how old.

Because Bella, Buddy, Lassie and Archie are – in their owner's eyes – without peer, beyond comparison. For each, their dog is The Best, Cutest, Fastest Dog. Even if our dogs seem to get along, that does not mean I must make small talk with you, be civil to you, greet you with the joy that our dogs greet each other. No, it is for The Animals to display those glorious, joyous emotions, not us Humans. No, I Human look down my nose at those other Humans, I do not have to chit-chat with them only because my Bella loves your Buddy. When my Beautiful Adorable Dog leaves a dump, I pick it up daintily with a baggie, making it appear as the most stylish and simplest of moves, not a rather disgusting task only done because everyone is watching.

Lastly, do not check out other Dog Owners, in the hopes of starting a flirtation. Even if our dogs get along and you look rather elegant and sexy in your Dog Park Gear, remember, we are only in the Dog Park because of our creatures, not for our vanity. Since there can sometimes be quite a conglomeration of Human Dog Owners in the Dog Park, it is recommended to not venture out in the sloppiest, unkempt outfit. Yes, it is only the daily dog walk, but no, do not walk out in your saggy jeans or drooping sweatshirt. Remember, there is Dog Park Social Etiquette.

April 2020

STOMACH TELLS THE TRUTH (INDIGESTION 1)

Despite our best efforts to suppress emotion, function with a cool head, override fear and anxiety, march forward as if nothing touches us – our body has a wonderful way of telling us, 'No, not this,' or 'No, this is no good.'

A dependable truth barometer is always the stomach.

The dinner invitation was half-hearted. More than a dinner invitation, a chance to show off her lifestyle (my new Mercedes car, my new house, my 2-year old daughter, my husband), I have it all, great career, great family life, everything money and love can obtain.

After surviving the first few hours in her company, it was evident that it was all appearances, a mirage, a fabricated construct which covered an unhappy marriage, an overworked woman and an emotionally disturbed child so distressed her perpetual constipation was a daily test of stewed plums and medicinals.

The kitchen was crowded with jars, flies, a semi-functioning stove, dust and oil smears covering most surfaces. No food was stocked, a guest had brought some frozen asparagus and a few last-minute snack purchases, which were briskly thrown together and brought to table as The Dinner Spread.

The garden was overgrown, trees, shrubs, grass waving wildly this way and that. In the middle, strewn over the lawn, was an earth mound with a shovel leaning over the edge, the landscaping project halted mid-air.

Husband came in wearing pants which seemed to have shrunk high above his ankles. He supplied one alcoholic beverage after another, until the guests could barely crawl home.

Upon boarding the train home, happy to flee this disaster scene, nausea overcame her and she had to get out midway, to unceremoniously throw up the dinner remnants behind a park shrub. Feeling as if she had been through a washing machine spin cycle, she boarded the next train, happy to get as far away from that nightmare dinner as was possible.

Years later, the divorce news came through. Her stomach had detected that correctly.

2011

WONDERFUL MORNING

The skies were blue and the sun shone brightly. A fresh breeze kept the temperature just right. First stop – charity shop, leave 3 sweaters, 1 shirt, 1 book and 1 sports item as donation.

Second stop – subway on way to work, above me on the escalator a young woman, pushing a baby buggy and surrounded by 3 dogs. Only when we got to the top did we see she was barefoot, her hair was a straggly mess, she wore just a light tank top and shorts. The dogs were not on leashes, had no muzzles, as the law requires on public transport. The baby buggy was filled with an assortment of bags, the dogs followed her quietly and obediently. She walked amongst the morning rush of people going to work as if she too were going somewhere important, not milling around aimlessly in the city.

Third stop – the hotelry and catering school, usually the teenagers about to enter the hospitality industry have to wear a uniform of black suit and white dress shirt, but today being Friday, they are wearing casual jeans, sneakers, their hair arranged in wilder looks. It is Casual Friday and they celebrate it.

Fourth stop – the kindergarden on the corner, teachers are already pushing buggies with their dozen wards, all little dwarves wearing orange vests, so they remain clearly visible in the crowd. The full buggy clatters around the corner, tiny voices all abuzz, they have a morning field trip.

Fifth stop – Rachel Whiteread's memorial of stone books in honour of the Jews killed over the centuries, above the spot where the first Jewish Schul was in 1421. Sixth stop – the pillow and linen shop, where the two women already sit at their sewing machine and table, material and needle flying through the air as they create more beautiful household textiles.

All that lies on my way to work, in the 1st floor law office with balconies lining the inside courtyard, to my Rapunzel Room. The onion and oil cooking stink from the restaurant below rising at 10am already, where I will hear that there are no two capitals or commas for "Kind Regards." No matter, the day is won already, I gathered all those visual telegram messages on the way, I am full and happy.

May 2021

KILL THE COCKROACH!

Ma & I walked into the health food store. By the first shelf, lying on the ground at our feet, lay a big brown cockroach, on its back, legs and antennae flailing. Two steps to the right was the saleslady behind the cash register desk.

"*Señorita*, look! There is a huge cockroach lying there, alive!" Ma yelled to the saleslady, finger pointing directly at the insect.

The saleslady calmly looked up, walked over to see what the fuss was about.

"*¡Mátala!* Kill it!" Ma ordered.

The saleslady slowly moved her foot over the cockroach, one of her Ugg-like, soft-soled boots covering the creature, smashing it and sliding it, still under the shoe, to her cash register desk.

"You should be fumigating, exterminating, spraying against them!" Ma exclaimed.

"They come from next door, the roast chicken place," the saleslady elaborated, "with our open shop front, they come into the neighbour as well. It is too difficult to control," she finished, resignedly.

Ma & I wandered through the shop, found our chia & ginseng and left without any further in-store cockroach sightings.

December 2021

2ND-HAND BRIDAL GOWN

The gown hung next to the shelf with shawls, tablecloths and knick-knacks, half-hidden by the column and skirt rack. Dozens of tulle petals covered the skirt, attached to a tight strapless corset, with a 3-meter long veil squeezed into the clotheshanger on which it was displayed. "Pronovias" was printed onto the thin ribbons sewn into the corset interior. The skirt ended in a mermaid tail shape, 2 meters of material to be trailed by the bride down the aisle.

Now the seam edges were grey and dusty, from the bride hopefully dancing all night, dragging her glorious gown through church, party venue, tables laden with well-wishing guests. Her day to shine, her princess entry, her childhood and teenage dream come true, running off with a prince and diamond ring on her finger. Her parents had been able to afford the bridal gown new, laying down a juicy sum of EUR 2.000 for it.

Some of her friends, not so well-off, had been snuck into the hidden room on the 2nd floor of the Used Clothing Bazar. There, at the back, was the Room of Used Bridal Gowns. For those young women unable to afford a new gown, this room was the answer. Married women had donated their once-worn bridal gowns, from years or months ago. The marriage ended quickly or after a dozen years, or no children followed, to receive the gown as a family heirloom and honour a tradition.

Online, 2nd-hand gowns of this brand were going for EUR 700, still a considerable investment. In the 2nd-hand shop, this glorious gown was priced at EUR 25, but that week before Christmas, there was an additional -50% discount, leaving it at a very affordable EUR 12.50. Even at this bargain price, the 3 bridal gowns found no buyers.

Was it that superstition, that a used gown would bring bad luck? The sweat stains in the underarm area might be a challenge to remove. Dry-cleaning alone would add up to EUR 100, costing far more than the dress itself. How much was one willing to pay, for a day of dreams, phantasies and princes?

December 2021

SOUND MIND, BROKEN BODY

My last two bosses were highly intelligent men with brilliant careers and dazzling fortunes, who had broken their bodies along the way. One decided to rock-climb as high as he could, unsecured, falling the equivalent of 4 floors, breaking many bones and lying in a hospital for months after. The other had run marathons and ridden horses until his heart stopped and his shoulder cracked. Both were in their 50s, both thought their superhuman strength would help them recover in no time. Both realised, after 2 years of intensive rehab, that their brain had been affected in such a way, that not even 10 years of intensive rehab would help. Nothing would ever bring them back to their previous mental acumen.

After their extreme body tragedies, both these Alpha men mixed up names and numbers. Their tempers became irregular, swinging between joy and anger, manifested in outbursts of gentle humour or hostile aggression. Their agendas were no longer chock-a-block full with appointments, their energy level fell to 1/10th of what it was. They could not match faces to names. They fell to pontificating and talking about "the good old times," reminiscing that time when their bodies could be pushed to the limit without any consequence.

It would not have been such a big deal, but for the fact that both men refused to yield, share, hand over some of their power and influence. None of their client accounts or billings were handed to a younger, more capable colleague. On the contrary, the two broken men clung to their Boss Chair, preferring to leave no business for the next generation, no office functioning without them. They clung on, going to every kind of physiotherapy, to regain that winning position they had unwillingly lost.

"Tomorrow is Saturday, do not come to the office," staff had to remind Boss#2. "You cited an hourly rate of EUR 280 for that client," Boss#1 had to be righted. Staying at home was not an option for them, they still had their ownership share in the office, could not be told to relinquish. A daily dance on eggshells for those who just wanted a monthly salary for doing the follow-up admin to these lead horses. Better to not push the body so far as to leave the mind struggling for direction amongst broken hearts and bones.

December 2021

51 IS AN OLD FLAME

The apple-upside down cake came out of the oven, neatly and perfectly, at 10am. Everything was ready for the birthday celebration, all that had to be done was wait for the guests. Two weeks earlier, repairing the gas oven cost EUR 300, almost the cost of a new oven. The two young repairmen had insisted on repairing the 10-year old oven, saying it was a good, solid model and still had a few more years in it.

It was to be a sales pitch, so they could pocket those EUR 300, because later that day, huge blue flame clouds appeared each time the gas pilot was lit. Then the grey metal surrounding one of the heaters started going grey, black, small spots appearing, smoke billowing up. The heat would not disperse, spreading further along the grey metal surface. To avoid a full-fledged kitchen fire, the gas feed was turned off, relegating all heating to the small microwave oven.

By the time the guests arrived, any celebratory spirit had literally gone up in smoke. No handyman answered the phone that Sunday afternoon, leaving any hope of repair or salvation pending for the next day, Monday, when people started functioning again. The birthday cake in the gas oven had caused a gas blow-out and for all the worry of getting it replaced, avoiding an entire apartment explosion, there was no more party.

December 2021

PAPER-THIN WALLS

Hearing neighbour coughing all night, then hearing of his death, realising those hacks were last breaths of dying man. Hearing painful coughing from apartment below, also during the night, hoping it will not also be a harbinger of upcoming death. Hearing Pa coughing, murmuring, sleep-talking, sighing, Ma snoring quietly, hoping they will also still be on this Earth for another few years, months?! The breath of life, coming across all walls.

In another city, the walls bring sounds of arguments – rebellious teenagers, lovers fighting, doors slamming, yelling, anguished cries and yelps. In one mailbox I left some articles on domestic violence, a few weeks of silence ensued. We live so close together in cities, piled atop and beside each other, doors and walls separate us in appearance only. We are human animals, roaming our urban cages, trying to not go under in the asphalt jungle.

January 2022

MILANO CRUDO

Because of my travel companion's odd appearance (2-meters tall, slightly overweight, heavy on the make-up woman colleague), we received the worst treatment during our Milan weekend. Salesladies would not attend us, coffee staff would serve the table neighbouring table and disparagingly ignore us, in an ice-cream shop she was served an extremely laden and absurdly drowned-in-whipped-cream-scoop, as if to mock her size and appetite.

The only pizza we had in a restaurant was from the freezer, not even properly heated up in the oven, half-raw, the dough still white and chewy. In another restaurant, they charged us every single item on the table – breadbasket, shot glasses filled with liqueur, snacks we never ordered, side dishes brought unordered – as if we were prisoner diners, forced to eat and pay whatever was laid on the table in front of us. When we argued over the exorbitant bill, we were told, "You had all of these items, they were on your table!" Absolute highway robbery.

When we finally boarded the bus taking us back to the airport, we hoped no one would push an unwanted invoice on us or completely ignore us. In the words of a gallerist friend, "a brutal city" indeed.

June 2006

KEEPING UP APPEARANCES

Pat gave outward appearances first priority. She had herself reelected for a second term as volunteer president (not really allowed), married a pilot to have free flights (jetset lifestyle), always wore red lipstick, operated her shortsightedness out for contact lenses (despite a first conjunctivitis attack, needing a second surgery), bought the latest fashion on her trips to San Antonio, Texas, started affairs with the boss and bragging her son spent New Years' Eve in New York City, where The Ultimate New Years' Celebration had to be.

Despite her best efforts, karma had a way of catching up. When her husband came to pick her up once from work, without his pilots' uniform, he was announced as her chauffeur (owing to his short stature and differing skin tone). When she was about to give her annual report speech, opening her wardrobe to pull out the newest dress, she realised with horror that one of her fired maids was so disgruntled, she left with the patrons' unworn dress. Pat would have to wear something "already seen," "already worn." Her son was run over by a snow removal truck, leaving him with lifelong fractures to recover from. Sometimes life was a great equalizer.

January 2022

AFFAIR OUT OF HAND

Many men think that having a little fling here or there is harmless. Their wife is comfortably installed in the house, plenty of opportunities present themselves in the workplace, why give up a bit of fun? They embark on affairs as if going to the gym for a little workout, squeezing it into their schedules as if it were a lunch appointment or client consultation. Most of the time, ending these affairs is easy, everyone having understood it is only a passing thing. A little stolen joy which had to end sometime.

The situation becomes hairy when one of the parties does not wish to end the affair, has somehow imagined it will lead to a life together, New Coupledom, L - O - V - E. If either party does not let go, hanging on, pleading, begging, stalking, then the Affair gets Out of Hand. This is the risk of having a bit of fun.

This lesson was learned by a famed medical doctor and a prosperous restauranteur. The first almost had to leave the country, leaving behind his angry wife and 5 children, a decades-long successful career, doctor's office in a top hospital. His bit of fun shot her husband, drove to the hospital, ran to him and begged him to save her. He locked her up in a patients' room and told authorities they could not see her because her state of health was too delicate. A few days later, she was imprisoned for 1 year, but due to her dead husband's great wealth, could bribe prison officials to supply her a better menu and let her wear tracksuits instead of the garish prison uniform. The doctor's wife had asked around, what did people think of that woman, "She is crazy" was what came back. The wife decided to stay with her doctor husband. She even outlived him, a bout of breast cancer not clearing the way for his other bits of fun.

The married restauranteur with a roving eye, courting his assistant, accountant, a few of his waitresses, was not discouraged by the debris left behind from his affair with his coiffeur's wife. Maggy had left Joey, asking Restauranteur to help her set up her new house of singledom. She did so in the hopes of snagging Lover for good. She would give him the children he wished for, which his wife had been unable to give, due to some youthful miniskirts worn in Winter leading to Fallopian tube infections. Maggy decorated her house as she thought Restauranteuer would like it, elegant curtains, large front- and backyards, a tasteful sculpture of a mother nursing a baby at her breast.

After a few months of visiting this Love Nest, Restauranteur got cold feet and retreated. By this time, his wife and their group of friends all knew of his gallivanting adultery. Half of their friends were on his side, the other side were on Maggy's side, a rift which would last through the decades and never mend. His wife forgave him, did not kick him out of their house.

It did not die down into a harmonious reconciliation. Wife reminded him almost every day of his failings, his flirtations, his infidelities. The breakfast table was the first battleground, ending with her coddling of the dog, as an *Ersatz*-child, the only presence she would allow in her bed. Restauranteur was banished to the guest bedroom.

When starting an affair, these long-term consequences were to be kept in mind.

January 2022

STOMACH TELLS THE TRUTH (INDIGESTION 2)

It was to be an afternoon dessert, small snack, brief visit, quick hello. It turned into a Party for 3 at 3, the hangover lasting for 4 days afterwards.

At first, it was one slice of apricot cake, a light biscuit dough, with a glass of prosecco. The slice which came along easily took up half the baking pan, drowned on the plate with a healthy dollop of whipped cream. 'Richard went especially early to the bakery, to get the freshest slices,' Vanessa said proudly. 'We only serve the day-of cake, no left-overs, nothing from yesterday or day before yesterday,' she clarified. 'Have another slice, more *Schlagobers*, I beat it myself, just now, all fresh, by hand, no electric beater,' Vanessa boasted.

After those two enormous cake slices with half a bowl of *Schlagobers* and two glasses of prosecco, came the ice cream. 'You must try at least a scoop, it is from the Italian on the corner, our favourite flavour, *stracciatella*, and more *Schlagobers*, we still have half a bowl left, it has to go, all of it, no use keeping it in the fridge after, it won't be good later,' Vanessa insisted. Richard dutifully brought out three bowls heaped with ice cream and *Schlagobers*, another glass of prosecco followed.

Even with sparkling conversation and wonderful travel anecdotes, it did take her stomach 4 days to recover from the excess. She stumbled home at 7pm, rather early, took 4 Alka Seltzers upon dizzyingly keeling into her own kitchen, somehow found her bed. The next 4 days were a diet of crackers and tea.

Lesson repeated painfully, never good to override the stomach telling us, 'Enough! Stop! No more!'

June 2020

BLIND

On my sister Anja's 49th birthday, I went to a classical music concert. It was an afternoon rehearsal with tickets for sale, the first 12 rows of seats remaining empty to allow the orchestra a peaceful practice session.

The music soared across the empty rows, to the crowds seated at the back. Up in the balcony, a husband and his blind wife sat, listening attentively. He sat in the row behind her, laying his hand on her shoulder when she sought him out. Either she leaned her head back, as if looking for him on the ceiling, or her hand looked for his on her shoulder.

They both must have been in their 70s, if not 80s. They inhabited their own world. Her navy blue jacket matched the pants, a light-blue striped blouse covered no bra. Not a drop of make-up, no jewelry, hair combed back austerely. The husband dressed and cleaned her as he would himself, her appearance was a twin image of his own, the bare minimum. On her right arm, above the elbow, was a yellow band with 3 black dots, informing passers-by of her blindness.

During the concert, she rocked gently back and forth, hands spread out flat on her lap.

During the quarter-hour pause, she sat patiently, ears alert to all sounds of people shuffling about, doors opening and closing, chairs scraping the floor. Her husband sat hunched over a game of Sudoku, thankful for the few minutes he was able to not have to focus entirely on his wife's needs.

How many people lived in these small bubbles of family carer for an ill, ageing, fragile partner or relative? The cocoon around them woven thicker each day, until only the 2-3 people in it could communicate, only they followed every breathing moment of their loved one. There was no more going out, no more socialising, no more sharing activities with friends in restaurants or movies. If she was blind, she depended entirely on her husband to guide her. Listening to the concert, her mind could travel to those years when she was young, beautiful, active. Now, the Autumn of her years, everything moved at snails' pace and energy was something to be portioned in little bits for each hour.

Was Anja telling me that soon I would be taking care of Pa and Ma in this way? That it is all bearable and patience springs eternal? Butterfly on my shoulder, soft wings flapping

gently, reassuring me that life has its ways and
to not despair.

May 2022

GENDER POLITICS RUIN DINNER

The restaurant dated back to 1740, claiming to be one of the oldest in town. Tourist hordes flocked to the end of the tram line, filling two long buildings and two outdoor patios. Once a month, the Canadian Expats met there, welcoming newcomers and greeting old friends. The waiting staff knew this table, knew they could swell to 20 guests, knew they were good business.

That evening, the two women taking care of the fresh food buffet had fallen out with the two men serving beverages. The experienced male waiters were letting the newbie women waitresses flounder, flail and fail. A long line of 12-15 hungry guests hopped from foot to foot, craned their neck towards the bright buffet vitrine, chit-chatted with their queue neighbour. A tipsy regular growled at the ladies waiting in line, „Da ya know what ya want?!" chuckling at his own double-entendre.

Minutes went by, 5, 10, 15. A woman waitress was running back and forth between buffet cash register and a guest table, long paper bill flapping. „You did not punch it in correctly!" one of the male waiters growled openly at her. The other male waiter approached me, „If you want something from the menu, we'll bring it to the table." Everything in the menu was breaded and fried – breaded mushrooms, fried Brie, fried potato croquettes. Salads, fresh bread, cheeses and cold cuts were only available in the buffet vitrine. „No, thank you," she said, she would wait for the buffet. 20 minutes, 25. That was it, she was going hungry, giving up. A soda drink and then get out as quickly as possible.

The waiter later brought 4 plates of breaded and fried items to the other Canadian Table guests. He knew he had lost business for 2 guests, not even a dent in his earnings. Certainly she would never go back there, pity those gender politics and the earning of tip money had soured what could have been a nice evening.

October 2022

CALLING ALL CATS

The building janitor was a stooped man with white hair, shuffling between floors and basement, collecting trash, sweeping, mopping up, taking care of pets and plants when tenants travelled for longer periods. He was Turkish, talking through the fence with the Turkish Consulate staff next door. They supplied him with tax-free cigarettes, one pack per day was his pace. His sky-blue eyes registered every entrance and exit, every car, every visitor, every discarded item.

His son had the same piercing sky-blue eyes, the same generous spirit, the same skill of observing and repairing. Where the father was a Napoleon-size, the son was Greek god-size. Strong, muscles bulging in all the right places, towering over most mortals. After his engineering degree, he set up his own construction company. He could walk into any property, assess the weaknesses and calculate repair costs within a few minutes. Brilliant analytical eye.

Upon visiting one apartment to estimate a balcony screen, he chanced upon the domestic cat. „Ah, kitty kitty kitty," he chirped. He bent down and tried to touch the cat, which fled into the next room. „I know a trick," this giant said, „I tested it during my Summer holiday in

Turkey, it worked, suddenly I was surrounded by dozens of cats, from the whole town, they all came out to see where the miaowing was coming from!" he boasted. He placed his cellpone against a doorjamb, googled a video on Youtube and played it. Cat calls sprang out of the phone. The domestic cat slowly tiptoed over to the phone, ears alert, wondering where those cat calls came from, entranced. „It is probably a mother cat calling her kittens," Engineer said. A mother's call always brought her kittens to her, even if coming out of a cellphone. A tall engineer with a soft spot for kitty cats.

October 2022

CALLING ALL GOATS

French Jean-Baptiste was a picture of Gallic elegance. Aquiline nose, luminous green eyes, flashing smile displaying a wonderfully straight row of teeth. Medium height, nicely proportioned, sharp mind, dry sense of humour, loyal to his sweetheart Carmine. In the office he went by „JB."

One afternoon, Julia and Janet reviewed daughter Sophie's homework. They were plowing through Greek mythology, learning about creatures with 2 dog heads or 7 snake necks, lion claws or bulls with human bodies following red yarn through labyrinths. JB stopped in the office hallway, „Yes, I know about those goats, they ride away in chariots, flying across the skies, endowed with supernatural powers." Julia and Janet nodded agreement, wondering later, „Flying *goats* in chariots?" They must have missed that Greek myth?

„Mmm, exactly which myth is that, JB?" they ventured diplomatically. „All of them, they all have Greek *gods*, pronouncing the g-o-d-s as g-o-a-t-s. Julia and Janet stifled smiles as they realised the misunderstanding. Their visions of goats in flying chariots were far more amusing.

Almost a decade later, Formula 1 drivers wanted to be called goats, „G.O.A.T.S." The Greatest Of All Time. Lewis Hamilton was a

G.O.A.T. He was flying across space in his speedy chariot, blurring the line between human being and divine driver.

Julia and her daughter Sophie did join those Greek gods of mythology, leaving this Earth too early, too unexpectedly, a tear, a gap in their stead. Two brilliant women illuminating the night sky as stars now, they are The Greatest Of All Time too.

For Julia Whitworth & her daughter Miss Sophie

September 2022

CHICA TERREMOTO

October is earthquake season in Peru. One week before the due date, Ella and her husband Tulio went to the hospital for the routine check, pregnancy on track, mother and unborn baby doing fine. As they entered the hospital, everything started to shake. Earthquake Season was upon them. The whole building rattled, window panes collapsed, chairs and tables flew across rooms. Tulio bundled Ella under a table and ran to a doorway, hoping the shock would not cause a premature birth or miscarriage. Ella huddled under the table, praying. A week later, a healthy baby girl was born.

The strength of those earth-moving shifts went into that baby girl and she came out fierce and fearless. A few years later she wrapped cats up in linens and put chalk to their paws, teaching the pets to write. When visiting her older male cousins, she would chase them out of their hiding spots under the bed, waving broomsticks to and fro until they cowered behind their mother for protection. Her uncle recognised the indomitable spirit and called her „*Chica Terremoto*," „Earthquake Girl."

What this world needs is more Earthquake Girls!

For Milagritos
October 2022

ABOUT THE AUTHOR
Heinz Hermann Wilhelm Neuenhaus

Born 16 April 1914 in Wesel, Germany. Third of four children, he and younger sister Ilse (born 1919) are the little ones, oldest sister Lotte (born 1905) and brother Werner (born 1908) are the older ones.

Young Heinz (maybe 6 or 7 years old, photo 1920?) holds his brother and sister protectively, his right arm over his older brother's shoulder, his left hand on baby Ilse's shoeless, pudgy foot. Heinz's white sailor shirt is clean and ironed, these four children were the pride of their parents.

18 March 1928, Wesel
Teen Heinz (turning 14 in one month) in school
uniform? New suit?

Marries Elisabeth Luise Doehrn on 16 October 1939. Liz (born 24 January 1919 in Wesel) is the same age as Heinz's younger sister Ilse. Ilse and Liz are friends, possibly the way Heinz and Liz met? Ilse brought her friend over, introduced her older brothers?

October 1939
(perhaps 16 Oct,
their wedding day?)

June1940

Only son Joerg Neuenhaus born on 2 May 1941 (conceived September 1940).

Bansin, Germany, Summer 1942, Baby Joerg, Age 1

Died 20 August 1941 (age 27) as machine gun officer at Russian Front in Zapolotje. He knew of his firstborn son, Joerg, but never held or saw him.

Ihr Vater

Heinz Hermann Wilhelm Neuenhaus   Unteroffizier
geboren am 16.04.1914 in Wesel
Erkennungsmarke: -87- 12./ Infanterie-Regiment 453
Truppenteil: 4. Kompanie (Maschinen-Gewehr) Infanterie-Regiment 426

ist am 20.08.1941 in Dedowa-Luka/Russland gefallen.

Seine letzte Ruhe fand er in

Klimkowa/Russland, Kameradengrab 3 von links am Südausgang
hinter der Straße von Klimkowa nach Sabolotje

Über den heutigen Zustand der Grabstätte und ob diese noch existiert, liegen keine Auf-
zeichnungen vor.

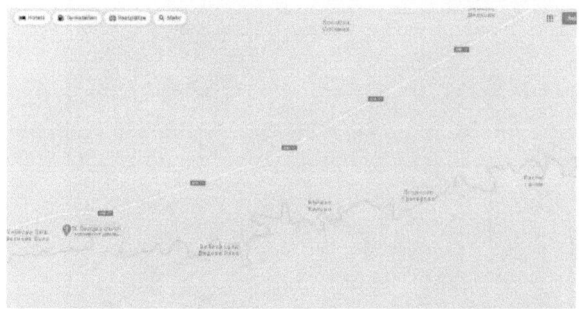

© 2021 Google Maps

Heinz's last letter

Heinz Neuenhaus 4./J.R.47.6
Eroeffnet Wesel, den 29. Oktober 1941
Amsgericht __inspekt. Als Rechtspfleger

Samstag den 21. Juni, 1941

Mein liebes Liesslein!

Morgen frueh werden wir die russische Grenze ueberschreiten. Die Kameraden sind eben abgerueckt, da will ich Dir auf alle Faelle ein Brieflein schreiben. Ich will nicht hoffen, dass dieser Fall eintritt, ja, ich weiss, dass er nicht geschrieben werden braeuchte. Trotzdem aber tue ich es, um auch in dieser Hinsicht Ruhe zu haben. Du, mein liebes Spatzele und unser Joerglein, Ihr seid meine Liebsten, die ich je hatte. Wenn ich auch unseren Bub nicht von Angesicht kenne, so weiss ich doch, dass er ein ordentlicher and strammer Kerl wird. Dafuer buergt aj schliesslich auch seine tuechtige Mutti, die fuer die richtige Erziehung sorgen wird. Ich weiss, dass alles in meinem Sinne geschieht, denn dafuer waren wir schon stets eine Person.

Ich will hier keine grosse Abschiedsrede schreiben, das ist bei uns nicht noetig. Etwas moechte ich aber noch als meinen besonderen Wunsch dazusetzen. Es ist selbtverstaendlich, dass alles was mir gehoert, auch Dein Eigentum ist. Denke daran, dass das

Sparkassenbuch in Duesseldorf das Kennwort „Topper" hat. Aber eins vor allem: Sollte ich tatsaechlich nicht zurueckkommen, so bleibe nicht Dein Leben lang Witwe. Du siehst es selbst an Mama, wie einsam es letzten Endes trotz eines Kindes ist. Ich brauche dazu nichts besonderes zu schreiben. Du verstehst mich auch so und weisst, aus welchen Motiven heraus ich zu dieser Meinung komme.

Ich muesste den letzten Teil doch noch im Gras schreiben, als es gestern Abend zu dunkel wurde. Aber fertig werden musste er. Ade, mein lieber Schatz und mein kleiner Joerg. Unser Zusammensein was das schoenste in meinem ganzen Leben.

Dein Heinzle!

Heinz Neuenhaus 4./J.R.47.6
Opened Wesel, on 29 October 1941
County Court __inspect. as judicial officer

Saturday 21 June, 1941

My Dear Lizzy!

Tomorrow morning we will be crossing the Russian border. The comrades have just disengaged, I most certainly want to write you a little letter. I do not want to imagine this case might come to be, yes, I know, that it does not need to be written. I do so regardless, to be at peace on this issue. You, my dear sparrow, and our little Joerg, you are my most beloved ones that I ever had. Although I have not seen him, I know that he will be a decent and strong boy. His capable mother will see to that, she will ensure a proper upbringing. I know all will be done in my conviction, since for that we were already one person.

I do not want to write a long farewell speech here, it is unnecessary when it comes to you and I. There is something I want to add as my special wish. It is understood, that everything I own is also yours. Keep in mind that the savings booklet in Duesseldorf has the password „Topper." But one thing over all: should I really not return, do not remain a widow your whole life. You see it yourself with Mother, how lonely it is despite having a child. I do not need to write anymore on that. You understand me just so and know, which reasons make me come to this conclusion.

I did now have to write the last bit in the grass, since yesterday evening it got too dark. But completing it needed. Adieu, my dearest darling and my little Joerg. Our union was the nicest part of my entire life.   Your Heinzle!

Footnote: Did he use the codename Topper for the joint bank account in honour of the 3 movies involving a shy and bumbling bank manager by the same name? Did he and Liz go to the cinema in Germany to watch Cary Grant and Constance Bennett doing crazy antics, playing ghostly tricks on serious banker Topper? Imagining Heinz and Liz as teenagers in the cinema, laughing with these Hollywood movies is a far happier picture than how it ended - too soon, too young, too incomplete.

3 Topper movies:

1937 – Topper

1938 – Topper Takes A Trip

1941 – Topper Returns

Ich möchte den letzten Teil doch noch zu Ihnen schreiben, ... es
jeden Abend zu dunkel würde. Aber fertig werden müßte ...
... mein liebstes ... und mein kleiner Junge, ...
... für das Glück in meinem ganzen Leben

            Dein ...

BIRTH CERTIFICATES

A.

Nr. 444

Borbeck, am 9. Mai 1885.

Vor dem untergeichneten Standesbeamten erschien heute, der Perſönlichkeit nach

———————————————————————— bekannt,

der _Bäckermeiſter Anton Schiebout van Gent,_ ————

wohnhaft zu _Kirchop Sedim s. 112_ ————

———————— _katholiſcher_ Religion, und zeigte an, daß von der _seiner Ehefrau Catharina Leaſe van Gent geborenen Schiffers,_ ————

———————————— _katholiſcher_ Religion,

wohnhaft bei ihm, ————

zu _Kirchop in seiner Wohnung_ ————

am _sechsten Mai_ ———————— des Jahres

tauſend acht hundert achzig und fünf ———— _Nachmittag_ =

um ———— _fünf un halb_ Uhr ein Kind _männ_ lichen

Geſchlechts geboren worden ſei, welches ———— _die_ Vornamen

Franz Hugo ————

erhalten habe. ————

————————————————————————

Vorgeleſen, genehmigt und unterſchrieben

Anton van Gent.

Der Standesbeamte.

In Vertretung

Kövenry

135

No. 474

Borbeck, am 9. Mai 1885

Vor dem unterzeichneten Standesbeamten erschien heute, der Persönlichkeit nach bekannt

der Bäckermeister Anton Nikolaus van Gent,

wohnhaft zu Frintrop Section I N^r 82,
katholischer Religion, und zeigte an, dass von der Maria Catharina Louisa van Gent geborene Schiffgens, seiner Ehefrau, katholischer Religion, wohnhaft bei ihm, zu Frintrop in seiner Wohnung am sechsten Mai des Jahres tausend acht hundert achtzig und fünf Nachmittags um fünf ein halb Uhr ein Kind männlichen Geschlechts geboren worden sei, welches die Vornamen
Franz Hugo
erhalten habe.

Vorgelesen, genehmigt und unterschrieben
Anton van Gent

Der Standesbeamte
In Vertretung
Furmann (?)

No. 474 (474th birth of the year)

Borbeck, on 9 May 1885

Fore the signing official appeared today, person known as

the master baker Anton Nikolaus van Gent,

residing in Frintrop Section I N^r 82,
Catholic Religion, and notified, that from Maria Catharina Louisa van Gent born Schiffgens, his wife, Catholic Religion, living with him, in Frintrop, in his house

on the 6th May of the Year eighteen hundred eighty-five, in the afternoon at 5:30 a child of male gender was born, who received the first names
Franz Hugo

Read out loud, approved and signed
Anton van Gent

The Registrar
Representing
Furmann (?)

A.   Nr. 212

Wesel, am 7. Mai 1895.

Vor dem unterzeichneten Standesbeamten erschien heute, der

Persönlichkeit nach _____ er kannt,

der Gastwirth Johann Heinrich
Hermann Döhren
wohnhaft zu Wesel Cazinenstraße No 546.
_____ evangelischer Religion, und zeigte an, daß von der
Elisabeth Döhren geborene El-
gering, seiner Ehefrau _____
_____ evangelischer Religion,
wohnhaft bei ihm, _____

zu Wesel in seiner Wohnung _____
am _____ acht en Mai _____ des Jahres
tausend acht hundert neunzig und drei _____ Vormittags
um _____ sieben Uhr ein Kind weiblichen
Geschlechts geboren worden sei, welches _____ die Vornamen
Wilhelmina Henriette _____
erhalten habe .

_____

Vorgelesen, genehmigt und unterschrieben
Johann Heinrich Hermann Döhren

Der Standesbeamte.
In Vertretung:
Craemer

Die Uebereinstimmung mit dem Hauptregister beglaubigt,
Wesel, am 7 ten Mai 1895.

Der Standesbeamte.
I. Vertretung: Craemer

gestorben am 27.8.1905
in Neukölln
A Neukölln No 24/1905

No. 212

Wesel, am 4. Mai 1893

Vor dem unterzeichneten Standesbeamten erschien heute, der Persoenlichkeit nach bekannt

der Gastwirt Johann Heinrich Hermann Doehrn,

wohnhaft zu Wesel, Beguininenstrasse N⁰ 546, evangelischer Religion, und zeigte an, dass von der Elisabeth Doehrn geborenen Elgering, seiner Ehefrau, evangelischer Religion, wohnhaft bei ihm, zu Wesel in seiner Wohnung
am ersten Mai des Jahres tausend acht hundert neunzig und drei Vormittags um sieben Uhr ein Kind weiblichen Geschlechts geboren worden sei, welches den Vornamen
Wilhelmine Henriette
erhalten habe.

> *Vorgelesen, genehmigt und unterschrieben*
> *Johann Heinrich Hermann Doehrn*

> *Der Standesbeamte*
> *In Vertretung*
> *Craemer*

Die Uebereinstimmung mit dem Hauptregister beglaubigt
Wesel, am 4ten Mai 1893.

Der Standesbeamte
In Vertretung: Craemer

(Stamp in lower right corner, in blue ink, with handwriting: Gestorben am 27. August 1965 in Nierstein, lk 24/1965)

No. 212 (212th birth of the year)

Wesel, on 4 May 1893

Fore the signing official appeared today, person known as

the innkeeper Johann Heinrich Hermann Doehrn,

residing in Wesel, Beguininenstreet № 546, Evangelical Religion, and notified, that from Elisabeth Doehrn born Elgering, his wife, Evangelical Religion, living with him, in Wesel, in his house

on the 1st May of the Year eighteen hundred ninety-three, in the morning at 7:00 a child of female gender was born, who received the first names
Wilhelmine Henriette

Read out loud, approved and signed
Johann Heinrich Hermann Doehrn

The Registrar
Representing
Craemer

The accordance notarised with Main Registry
Wesel, on 4th May 1893.

The Registrar
Representing: Craemer

(Stamp in lower right corner, in blue ink, with handwriting: Died on 27 August 1965 in Nierstein, lk 24/1965)

A.

Nr. 204.

Wedel, am 22. April 1914

Vor dem unterzeichneten Standesbeamten erschien heute, der Persönlichkeit
nach _____
_____ bekannt,

der Metzger Wilhelm Heinrich
Neuenhaus,

wohnhaft in Wedel, Schmiedstraße 20,

_____ evangelischer Religion, und zeigte an, daß von der
Gertrud Margarete Emilie Neuenhaus
geborenen Hülser seiner Ehefrau
_____ evangelischer Religion,
wohnhaft bei ihm

zu Wedel in seiner Wohnung
am _____ fünfzehn ten April _____ des Jahres
tausend neunhundert und vierzehn _____ Vormittags
um ein ein halb _____ Uhr ein Knabe
geboren worden sei und daß das Kind _____ die Vornamen
Heinz Hermann Wilhelm
erhalten habe. _____

_____
_____

Vorgelesen, genehmigt und unterschrieben
Heinrich Neuenhaus

Der Standesbeamte.
In Vertretung
Beckmann

Die Übereinstimmung mit dem Hauptregister beglaubigt

Wedel, am 22ten April 1914

Der Standesbeamte.
In Vertretung Beckmann.

No. 204
Wesel, am 22. April 1914

Vor dem unterzeichneten Standesbeamten erschien heute, der Persoenlichkeit nach bekannt

der Metzger Wilhelm Heinrich Neuenhaus

wohnhaft in Wesel, Schmidtstrasse 28, evangelische Religion,
und zeigte an, dass von der Gertrude Margarete Emilie Neuenhaus, geborene Huelser, seine Ehefrau, evangelischer Religion, wohnhaft bei ihm,

wohnhaft zu Wesel in seiner Wohnung am 16. April des Jahres tausend neunhundert und vierzehn Nachmittags um vier einhalb Uhr ein Knabe geboren worden sei und dass das Kind die Vornamen Heinz Hermann Wilhelm
erhalten habe.

Vorgelesen, genehmigt und unterschrieben
Heinrich Neuenhaus

Der Standesbeamte
In Vertretung
Reckmann
Die Uebereinstimmung mit dem Hauptregister
beglaubigt

Wesel, am 22ten April 1914
Der Standesbeamte
In Vertretung Reckmann

No. 204 (204th birth of the year)

Wesel, (Wednesday) 22 April 1914

Fore the signing official appeared today, person known as

the Butcher Wilhelm Heinrich Neuenhaus

residing in Wesel, Schmidtstrasse 28, Evangelical Religion, and notified that, from Gertrude Margarete Emilie Neuenhaus, born Huelser, his wife, Evangelical Religion, living with him,

in Wesel in his house on 16th April of the Year nineteen hundred and fourteen afternoon, at 4:30, a boy was born – and the child received the first names Heinz Hermann Wilhelm.

Read out loud, approved and signed
Heinrich Neuenhaus

The Registrar
Representing
Reckmann

The accordance notarised with Main Registry
Wesel, on 22nd April 1919
The Registrar
Representing: Reckmann

A.

Nr. 24.

_ Moll am 25. Januar 1919.

Vor dem unterzeichneten Standesbeamten erschien heute, der Persönlichkeit nach _____

_____ bekannt,

die Ehefrau Milton Marie Pommer

wohnhaft in Moll Lerbmacher, Straße 17 _____

Religion, und zeigte an, daß von der

[illegible handwritten lines] ... Religion,

wohnhaft in Moll Lange Beginnenstraße

14,

zu Mülheim in Gegenwart der Anzeigenden

am ein und zwanzigsten Januar des Jahres

tausend neunhundert neunzehn _ Nach mittags

um halb ein halb Uhr ein Mädchen

geboren worden sei und daß das Kind _ die Vornamen

Elisabeth Luise Wilhelmine

erhalten habe.

Vorgelesen, genehmigt und unterschrieben

Marie Pommer _

Der Standesbeamte.

Ju Vertretung _
Reesmann

Die Übereinstimmung mit dem Hauptregister beglaubigt

Moll, am 25 ten Januar 1919

Der Standesbeamte.

Ju Vertretung: Reesmann.

Beglaubigt am 22 August 1985
in Mainz
St. A. Mainz   Nr. 1888/1985

Z. Nr. 1418

No. 24

Wesel, am 25. Januar 1919

Vor dem unterzeichneten Standesbeamten erschien heute, der Persoenlichkeit nach bekannt

die Hebamme Witwe Maria Pommer

wohnhaft in Wesel, Korbmacherstrasse 17
und zeigte an, dass von der Wilhelmine Henriette van Gent, geborene Doehrn, evangelischer Religion, Witwe des am 14. Oktober 1918 verstorbenen, zuletzt in Wesel wohnhaften Baecker Franz Hugo van Gent, katholischer Religion,
wohnhaft in Wesel, Lange Beguinenstrasse 14
zu Wesel...in Gegenwart von Anzeigenden am 24. Januar des Jahres tausend neunhundert und neunzehn Nachmittags um elfeinhalb Uhr ein Maedchen geboren worden sei — das die Vornamen Elisabeth Luise Wilhelmine
erhalten habe (xxx)

Vorgelesen, genehmigt und unterschrieben
Maria Pommer

Der Standesbeamte
In Vertretung
J. Reckmann

Die Uebereinstimmung mit dem Hauptregister beglaubigt

Wesel, am 25ten Januar 1919
            Der Standesbeamte
        In Vertretung J. Reckmann

(Gestorben am 22. August 1985 in Mainz, Nr. 1888/1985)

No. 24 (24th birth of the year)

Wesel, (Saturday) 25 January 1919

Fore the signing official appeared today, person known as

the midwife widow Wilhelm Maria Pommer

residing in Wesel, Korbmacherstrasse 17
and informed, that Wilhelmine Henriette van Gent, born Doehrn, Evangelical Religion, Widow of on 14 October 1918 deceased, lastly living in Wesel Baker Franz Hugo van Gent, Catholic Religion,
residing in Wesel, Lange Beguinenstrasse 14
in Wesel in presence of Notifier on (Friday) 24 January of the Year nineteen hundred and nineteen afternoon, at 11:30, a girl was born – receiving the first names of Elisabeth Luise Wilhelmine
(: stortenhaus 1. Woche gestrichen)

Read out loud, approved and signed
Maria Pommer

The Registrar
Representing
J. Reckmann

The accordance notarised with Main Registry
Wesel, on 25th January 1919
The Registrar
Representing J. Reckmann

(Died on 22 August 1985 in Mainz, Nr.
1888/1985)